Welcome To My Imagination

JOHN P ALBA

First Edition, 2014
ISBN: 978-0-9906878-2-5

Shield Blade Publishing
Buda, TX

Credits
Cover Art by Steven D Jones
Cover Design by John P Alba
Substantive and Copy Editing and by TL Jeffcoat

DEDICATION

To my family and friends for the encouragements of finally putting my imagination on paper.

CONTENTS

ACKNOWLEDGMENTS

I would like to thank the Twilight Zone TV show, Edgar Allen Poe, V C Andrews and the Great Stephen King for all the nightmares that helped me be afraid of day as well as night. A special thanks to my friend TL Jeffcoat.

All Up To You

If I were to disappear from yesterday would you remember me tomorrow? I have been gone so long that the only one that remembers me is me but only in dreams. Dreams are only the packaging of what you want, what comes out of the box is all up to you. I am tired of what was and what should have been and now I want to sleep and dream of nothing. I am tired of people not believing in what I say just because I am the one saying it. I just want to be left alone with my thoughts and they are the only thing I have left that believes me. I am tired of people not listening to me when all I want to do is rest so I can stop being me. I don't want to be a hero, I don't want to be a king, I don't want to be something I'm not, I just want to rest them where they can be free.

I am a beast, a monster, a creature of no importance that has been nowhere and hurt no one. I am a horrible person who cares for others and wishes that everyone finds friendship and happiness. I just wish I could be counted as a friend but it won't be the first time I'm not. In the memory of a dream, I was once considered real but now I'm just a memory of what I use to be and sometimes not even at all. I know I am a hated thing, I was content but now I am that which people hate and are ashamed of. I'm a regret from the past that has brought me here and I am the truth that everyone wishes was a lie.

THE BROKEN STAR RANGER

Twenty hands belonging to brown uniformed cadets are waved down by their Captain in the front of the classroom. The Captain straightens out a wrinkle in his shirt that must have escaped his wife's starching while the claps sputter on randomly for a few seconds.

I shift in my wheelchair while taking in the scene with amusement. I know the cadets should have been better disciplined than that but that is no longer my problem to deal with and has not been for many years. My old legs are no longer strong enough to hold me up without shaking like a soaked puppy that came out of a winter rain. The doctor never gave a clear answer as to what was wrong with my legs without mumbling all those long foreign doctor words anyway. What does it matter? I know what is wrong with my legs. I am just too damn old to stand anymore.

A few unruly cadets are clapping as the Captain steps behind the podium at the head of the classroom. I shake my head at the youngsters these days. After the second Great War the kids seemed more rebellious than back in my day. Maybe it is all the new automobiles they get to drive around in. I didn't drive till I was almost retired from the force. Spoiled is what the kids of today are.

"Settle down." The Captain commands.

My gaze drifts towards the two young men doing a two fingered golf clap on their wrists. I have no doubt they are excited to complete their training and become Texas Rangers soon but not enough sense to realize when they are pushing their luck.

"Tomorrow is the day that you will graduate from this sixty year old building in which thousands of rangers has trained. Y'all should be proud to be among those classes of the past. The sad news is that you twenty will be the last to graduate from this facility. After graduation at seventeen hundred hours tomorrow, these doors will be closed and this will no longer be the Texas Rangers training academy. The good news is that we have a guest speaker. His name is Captain Jacob Baker and he is the last of the ten Texas Rangers that first graduated from this place. Now let's give him the proper salute he deserves. Attention!"

All eighteen of the men and two women jump to their feet and raise hands to their heads in salute.

My arms ache as I push the tire bars and roll towards the podium. They are the strongest part left of me. I pull up to the side of the podium and try not to grumble like an old man does at children because everyone here is a child to me.

"All right sit down. Sit down! My neck hurts when y'all stand at attention like that." My voice requires no microphone which has left most of the front row wide eyed. I get that a lot.

The cadets sit and the room quiets. My old cheeks stretch with a smile. So many young faces and more than a few are looking at me with awe. Others are smug or could that be confidence? Do they believe they are really in the presence of someone who was once important? Or are they just proud of me for living so long? Either way they will never forget me after today.

At this age it is difficult to tell which is more shocking

to people, that I was a real Texas Ranger or that I am still alive. I never met that fellow on TV named Charles but he did not sound much like a real Ranger. He was always running around and kicking people in the head. Real Rangers shoot the bad guys or handcuff them. All that kickboxing nonsense was not much use against a bullet.

"I hope y'all are proud of yourselves because you'll carry on prestigious careers as Texas Rangers. You have the same look in your eyes I had the day I graduated. I know that being here shows your dedication to how tough y'all have trained but make sure however tough you are on the outside that you stay soft in the inside. The toughest of you will be tested in your careers just like I was many times. You are the best of what we stand for so be proud and remember your training."

I nodded to the Captain to let him know I am done with my opening before turning back to the cadets. "Are there any questions?"

A blond woman in the front row raises her hand. "Women were not allowed to think they could hold a law enforcement position when I was training." I say before she can ask her question. "Things changed in the years after all the young men traveled overseas to fight the Nazi's. I am proud that women hold such positions. What's your name?"

She jumps to her feet with her arms at her sides. "I'm Cadet Jenkins, sir! I'm ranked sixth in my class, sir!"

"I'm retired Cadet Jenkins. I'm not an officer so I'd like to ask you not do that. I never was a fan of all those formal military proceedings." Not to mention having perfectly good hearing as well. I poke a wrinkled finger in my ear to silence the ringing.

The cadets' heads shift towards the Captain who opens his mouth to talk but not before I establish my place as the speaker.

"I have the floor so don't pay no attention to him. There was a time when he was a cadet just like y'all and in those days he had a nickname. What was it? Oh yes…" My cheeks have not stretched this much from grinning in years. The Captain stares at me with wide eyes and flushing cheeks. "Don't you worry Catfish. I heard about your misdoings all the way to the panhandle. I won't tell them the story that I heard of your last week before graduation."

The cadets glance at the Captain and more than a few let a laugh slip. The Captain's brows lower and he clears his throat. "Eyes front!"

The cadets regain control of themselves in an instant. They watch as Captain Catfish and I stare at each other. The Captain laughs and I cannot hold back my own laugh in return. Then a few of the cadets snicker but turn serious as the Captain glares at them.

After the laughter dies, I return my attention to the blue eyed young woman sitting in front of me. "You wanted to ask me something sweetie?"

Flashing her perfectly squared teeth warms my heart. "What was it like to be a Texas Ranger when they rode horses? Did you meet any famous cowboys?"

Youngsters always start with the horse question. "So you want a cowboy story. Well okay. Sit back and get comfy while I tell you the story that led me to dream of becoming a Texas Ranger."

The ache in my chest is as fresh and painful today as it was so long ago.

"Cowboys, yeah I met a few of them and most were good but plenty were cattle rustlers, gamblers, and gunfighters. You hear all about the bad ones and some of the good ones."

Knots form in my gut as I dig through memories for the man that set me on the path to becoming a Ranger. "I know you've never heard of this gun-slinger. He was a strange lawman that showed up when I needed him. He was dressed like a Texas Ranger but his badge was missing the top point. He said it was a bullet that done it.

"He was tall of course at that time everyone was tall to

5

me. I was about eight or nine years old I believe. I still remember the events very well. I never knew his name which was strange because back then every lawman was always trying to get in the papers. They always went after the gunfighters with the biggest reputation. Many of them did make the papers but more in the obituaries instead of the front page.

"This cowboy changed everything for me and I made it through that sad part of life because of him. I was convinced to dedicate my life to being a Texas Ranger. If he wasn't really a Ranger I don't care. He saved me, my family, and possibly the whole town.

"I've told this story several times but I can't prove that he ever existed. I never heard another story about him.

"'I'm the last alive that remembers the cowboy. So I'll tell you this story so that he will not be forgotten. I want to be remembered long after I am gone for all the great things I have done. I want people to say that I made a difference in their lives like this Broken Star Ranger did for me."

~~~~~~~~~~~~~~~~~~~~~~~

Grayson T Sanderson and I were the best of friends but most people called him Gray. We were supposed to be fishing for crawdads but the water was too tempting so we did a lot more swimming than fishing.

The day was hotter than usual with no clouds and no breeze. We did not mind as we kept on swimming while catching a crawdad here and there. At least until we saw that the sun was already drifting behind the trees and the shadows had stretched across the river like shadowy wood spirits.

After counting the crawdads we agreed there were plenty. Then we dumped them back in the water so we could catch them again tomorrow.

We put on our shoes and raced home that day. I was always the fastest. It was five acres from the creek to my family's letterbox. Looking back as I reached it I saw Gray a little way behind me. So I waited for him.

After Gray caught up he bent over panting for a few minutes before smiling. We shook hands three times and then stomped our right foot. Two years ago we made this secret handshake for our friendship. He and I had planned to do it the rest of our lives, just between us.

"We meetin' again to catch some crawdads tomorrow?" Gray asked.

After I nodded, he ran off to the top of the hill between our homes. It was another ten acres to his house from the hill. I felt a little guilty for making him run so hard when he had so far to go but someday running all that way will make him as fast as me. As I walked down my driveway I realized how tired I was. I had to remind myself to stop dragging my feet.

You could say my house had seen better days. The roof had more patches than my clothes. We were not rich but we had each other and that is all that really mattered to us.

Pa was a hard working farmer. He always made sure we had food on the table, clothes on our backs, and that the bills got paid on time. Sometimes the food was not all that good but we always thanked God for what we had to eat. You better believe that one way or another he always made sure I did my schoolwork.

Pa was a good farmer like his father before him and his father's father before him. He told me he did not want me to be a farmer and that is why he pushed the education thing on me. He wanted me to use my brain instead of my back.

Ma was a good wife to Pa and a loving mother to me. She was kind but you did not want to get her riled up. She grew up tougher than her two brothers. She could shoot a snake in both eyes at ten paces with one eye closed and standing on a single leg. Although Pa bragged that he taught her how to shoot properly, Ma and I knew the truth.

Every once in a while he would come home broke after

drinking and gambling. He would sit in front of the house because he was not allowed in until he sobered up. It did not happen that often but maybe four or five times that I can remember. He learned how tough Ma was. She would wake him early the next morning by banging pots together or throwing water on him. Not surprising to anyone that he was always sorry the next morning.

Yeah he loved her and she loved him even when times were tough. They always found time to sit and tell each other how bad it would be without each other. No matter what happens they would always be there for me.

I could smell dinner when I approached the door. The sun was setting and the clouds looked like streaks of blood spread across the blue. The thought made me feel uneasy so I went on in and sat at the table where Ma was putting the last dinner plate down.

I was real hungry after crawdad fishing and I forgot my manners. I reached across the table to grab a biscuit before I noticed Pa's gaze on me. I did not realize the expression he had given me was a warning but I knew I had done wrong after a wooden spoon came down from behind me and slapped my hand.

Ma had placed the butter dish and was standing over me.

"You know that we pray first, son." She said.

"Sorry Ma. Can I say grace?"

She nodded, I prayed, and then we ate. I helped Ma clear the table once everyone was done while Pa went outside to smoke. Pa did not smoke often because money was scarce. The last crops had sold really well so we had a little left over. Pa was excited to have spending money.

After helping Ma I sat on the porch and enjoyed the cool summer night.

Pa sat in his rocker and told stories of how his father was always whooping on him and how Grandpa was "...meaner than a rattlesnake with a broken tooth and meaner than a nagging wife."

"What was that?" Ma called from inside the house.

Pa smiled at me and replied. "I love you dear wife."

I laughed until I saw a horse pulling a little wagon along our driveway, barely visible in the moonlight. I knew who it was in an instant. I ran to Grandpa before he could unclasp the horse and tie it to the porch.

"Why were you always whooping on my Pa and mean to him?" I am not sure why that came out of my mouth but I sure loved the answer.

His gray eyebrows rose and nearly touched the shaggy gray hair hanging from his head. His rough voice shook as he waved his hands while explaining it all to me.

"I whooped on him because he threw rocks at the horses, chased the chickens, threw their eggs, scared the horses, and ate your Grandma's pies before supper. Did he tell you about all those things he did to get a whooping? How would you like it if it was your birthday and someone ate your special pie?"

I laughed hard as we walked to the porch where Pa had given up his rocking chair so Grandpa could sit.

A few stories about Pa and Grandma and I was beginning to doze off. I gave them all hugs and kisses. I started to step inside when I smelled smoke. Pa's nostrils flared and he squinted as he smelled it.

Pa ran to the back of the house and I followed right behind thinking a fire had caught in the fields. Nothing was burning there so we ran to the front of the house to find Ma pointing up the road. Just beyond the hill was an orange glow that came from the direction of Gray's house.

Pa ran past almost knocking me to the ground. I followed him the instant I got my footing. My heart pounded in my ears as I imagined Gray helping to carry buckets to the fire.

I got to the top of the hill and Pa was already at the burning house. I could hear him hollering for Mr. Sanderson. The house was completely consumed by fire by the time I arrived at their barn. My heart sank into my stomach as the fire raged higher into the air. I felt the heat as the flames spread into the grass. The bushes by the windows popped and snapped inside the inferno. There was no way for anyone inside to escape the hungry flames. The roof of the house was already sinking.

As I passed in front of the barn I heard a horse snort and someone chuckle.

"Say goodbye to your friend." A rough and uncaring voice mocked me

Before I saw who spoke I was knocked down by something large and fuzzy. In the moonlight with flames roaring behind him was a man on a dark horse. As he turned his head from me his eyes glowed red. In that instant I knew this was all wrong. This was no accident. That red glow was not a reflection because he was between me and the fire. I stayed down as he galloped into the night.

Through the tears I watched my one true friend's home torn down by fire. More neighbors joined in and carried buckets from the well. In the end it was no use because no matter if I was ready to accept it or not I knew it was over for me and Gray.

The house that we played marbles and jacks in last winter was a skeletal frame of smoldering wood. The burning roof scattered the crackling frame that had begun to lean.

I saw them carry his body from of the wreckage. It was small and blackened like a grilled fish.

Ma tried to cover my eyes to what was my friend but I saw how bad he was burned. His dangling arms were blackened bone. His skin was gone and his muscles turned to ash.

I dove around Ma's arms and ran as fast as I could to where they were carrying away my best friend. "Get up Gray! Don't you give up! Get up!"

Pa's iron-like arms caught me before I could reach my best friend. I fought to escape but Pa held me tight to his chest. The smell of smoke and sweat on his clothes made the emptiness inside me deeper.

I cried out as I reached for him. "No! You can't be dead. This is a bad dream. Please get up! Please get up! We have to catch some crawdads tomorrow! You promised me! You promised me! We never break promises! We shook on it! Now get up!"

Pa held me tight to him and tried to soothe me. "I know it hurts son. I know it does." He whispered in my ear.

It took several minutes for me to regain my senses and when I did I remembered the stranger in the barn. "Pa! There was a man in the barn. He was laughing and knocked me down with his horse and rode away."

"I know you're upset but you can't make up stories."

Dragging him along by his sleeve, I pointed at the horse shoe prints by the barn. Everybody knows that Mr. Sanderson had no horses in the barn because it was too rickety to hold anything that could kick it over. His mind worked it over as he stared at the prints and gazed into the night where they disappeared.

"Sheriff!" Pa ran to where the sheriff was looking at the bodies.

The sheriff stood and caught him by the shoulders. I ran as close as I could before Ma grabbed me by the shirt. She did not want me to get too close to the carnage.

"You need to look into what started this fire. Someone was in the barn when it started."

"Mr. Baker, calm down. It was probably just the fireplace left unattended. Don't let your imagination get out of control. Nobody else saw anyone near the barn."

"Bullshit. It's the middle of the summer and there ain't no need to light the fireplace."

The sheriff leaned in close to Pa. I couldn't hear what was said but whatever it was Pa's cheeks burned red and he frowned. He did not push the sheriff any further. He turned and walked to Ma and I as Grandpa came over the hill in his wagon with a lantern hanging from the horse's straps to light his way.

We climbed onto the wooden bench hanging on the back of the wagon. Grandpa hummed quietly to himself as we returned home.

As we reached our driveway, Pa turned and kissed Ma and then pushed my head up with a finger under my chin. He brushed moisture from my filthy cheeks "I have a friend that's in the Texas Rangers. It's be a couple days before I hear back but I'll wire him in the morning before they bury the Sandersons."

We buried Gray the next day at noon. Everybody came to our house afterwards to mourn the Sandersons. I went to the old tree stump behind the house to dig up the box of stuff we buried there two months ago.

After months of saving up our pennies to buy the box, we brought it here. It was about as big as a hat box but it was heavy. The man at the general store said it was waterproof and durable. The only thing it needed was a lock for the sliding latch.

We were going to add stuff to it as we got older and in our old age we would open it and reminisce of all the things we did. This day I put the memory of my best friend in it. I promised to always remember him. There would be a day someone else would add all my memories to the box.

I went to the creek where Gray and I were crawdad fishing a day ago. Laughing and running in the water as we tried catching as many of the critters as we could. Today I sat on the edge of the banks throwing stones in the water. Anger was building inside of me and the only way I felt I could deal with it was to throw stones as fast as I could.

I threw handfuls upon handfuls of pebbles, stones, twigs, dirt, and pieces of driftwood. I cannot remember when I started crying. When I was about to wipe my tears I hesitated while looking at my hands. Little drops of blood had escaped the small cuts on my fingers. The anger had numbed the pain and I didn't care.

I laid in the dirt and watched the clouds pass by. I wasn't thinking of anything in particular when a strong cool breeze came through the trees. I thought I heard Gray running and laughing in the water. I wiped the tears and I somehow knew it was Gray telling me he was keeping his promise.

I ran and laughed, forgetting the pain and loss for a moment. After a few minutes my tears were gone and I was happy. Gray and I were playing as we always had.

We ran and played until the sun set and I knew Ma would begin to worry.

"Gray! Race you!"

I ran as fast as I could all the way to the letter box and then waited for Gray to get there but with a lump in my throat I remembered he was not coming. I cried for a while and then ran home. I missed him but I knew he was there in my heart.

I swung the door open and found my parents sitting at the table waiting for me. Their faces had been tight with worry but the tension was immediately gone when they saw me. They hugged me when they saw my puffy red eyes. They told me how much they loved me and would not know what to do if something bad had happened to me.

"Are you hungry?" Ma asked.

"Can I lie down?" Eating was the last thing I wanted to do right now. I was upset and my body felt as if it had been dragged behind a horse. The fatigue was pushing me to close my eyes while I was still on my feet.

"Okay son. If you change your mind then I'll fix you something."

"I love you." They both added after kisses and hugs.

"I love you too."

After changing into my sleeping clothes, I stared through the open window by my bed. I counted the stars which always helped me fall asleep. A cold wind blew in and clouds rolled across the sky. The clouds blotted out the light from the moon and stars to leave the sky nearly pitch black, except for lightning flashes webbing under the clouds and illuminating the underbelly of the giant gray puffs.

I heard no thunder but I closed the window in case the big storm came this way. The thunder began rolling as the clouds brought the storm with them. I pulled my blanket tighter and eventually I was asleep.

The next morning I woke covered in sweat and had to steady myself by holding the bed post. The room was spinning and it made my rumbling stomach lurch.

Images of a giant horse chasing me flashed in my mind. "Where are you, Gray? Where are you?"

Pushing away the nightmare, I ignored the dizziness and got dressed. Then I washed my face in the bucket we kept for cleaning ourselves.

The moment I stepped into the kitchen a pain shot through my stomach as I smelled sizzling bacon, eggs frying, and hot buttermilk biscuits baking. I was in breakfast heaven.

Pa entered the kitchen from the backdoor. "Hurry up and eat cause I need to go into town and I need you to help carry stuff. I might let you drive."

Torn between relaxing and enjoying the breakfast or getting a chance to drive the horses, I decided on both and crammed more food into my mouth than I could chew. I did not want to sit around today and be depressed.

Pa finished tying the horses as I swallowed the last bite. He let me drive. Each time I tried to pick up speed, he would pull the reigns to slow to a trot. I could have run faster but I did not argue because it gave us a chance to talk.

We stopped in front of the General Store and Pa went inside to get the things he needed. I waited outside by the wagon to watch every passerby and make sure they did not steal anything. A stagecoach stopped in front of the Post

Office across the street. A dusty bearded stranger stepped down.

His squared stance had me convinced he could chew rocks and spit sand. His black raincoat covered most of his body except for the black leather boots with silver spurs. His black hat was tilted so that only his brown short cropped beard was visible. He turned in my direction and I caught a glimpse of a revolver tucked in his belt. Underneath the raincoat were jeans, an off white shirt, and a brown vest.

I felt like his hard eyes were boring into my soul. Chills ran along my spine as I saw the scar in the center of his brow. It was pink and round. As he squinted at me it dimpled inward like a third eye.

With his back straight, he turned and walked around the stagecoach where a black horse was tied. He pulled the reins free and led the horse down the road towards the Sheriff's Office. He tied his horse to a post and scanned the street. His boots clicked across the wooden patio as he went inside. I tried not to stare at the horse or in that general direction after his heavy footsteps disappeared inside the two story building with barred windows but I could not help myself.

A few minutes later Pa was beside me. "It'll be a couple of hours before the clerk gets all the stuff ready."

"Pa, I just saw a big tall dark stranger go to the Sheriff." I whispered.

Pa glanced at the building as the man emerged from the shadows of the sheriff office. He pulled a gold disc from of his vest pocket and pinned it to his coat. The light reflecting off that thing had to be the brightest I had ever seen.

As he turned, the reflection shifted away and I realized it was a lawman badge. Unlike all the other badges, this one had four of the five points inside the circle. The top point was missing.

Pa approached him with a question. Maybe he knows

who Pa had sent for. The dark ranger shook his head but I could not hear his answer. Pa then waved me over.

I walked to them, glancing at our wagon as often as I could without walking into a wagon or horse. Pa patted my shoulder "I'm watching the wagon, son. Tell the Ranger what you saw."

I told him about the rider in the barn that had laughed and knocked me down. I was compelled to speak. Almost as if he had somehow willed me to tell him every detail from that night. The ranger listened without blinking.

"I will bring justice." The Ranger spoke with a deep rough voice.

He tipped his hat to us and then climbed onto his horse. The ranger rode off in the direction of the Sanderson's place. I could barely contain my excitement at the idea of him going straight to Gray's house.

"There's some things here in town I wanted to do. Is it okay if I stay? I'll walk home later."

"That's fine but be home for supper." In other words, don't be late or Ma would be waiting with a switch for making her worry.

I ran all the way to Gray's house. As I reached the scorched front yard, my chest burned from the quick huffs. My eyes watered from the ache in my side which felt as if I had been punched in the liver. As soon as I could control my breathing and stand upright without the world spinning I searched for the ranger.

He was crouching and inspecting the fading hoof prints near the barn. I ducked low to sneak up behind him like when Gray and I used to catch jackrabbits in the woods. I made no sound stalking on my toes. This was much easier than chasing those furry creatures that neither Gray nor I had ever actually come close to catching.

"He was your best friend, wasn't he?" The Ranger spoke without turning from the barn.

I stopped ten feet from him, so much for being easy.

"Yes he was." Saying 'was' only reminded me that Gray was no longer here. It is strange how a simple word could make my heart ache.

"The man that did this will pay for what he took away."

He stood and turned to me with a grim expression. His eyes were dark and determined. He took off his hat but his face seemed to remain in the shadows. Then he gave my shoulder a reassuring squeeze with his large hand.

"I promise this and I never break a promise." His voice was rough and deep as if his throat was coated with dirt from the years of riding across arid hot lands.

I placed my hand into his leathery palm and he shook it three times and then stomped his right foot. I gaped at his foot. How did he know? Who could have told him? I opened my mouth but before I could ask, he answers. "A friend of yours sent me."

I stood there with my mouth hanging open. I tried to find the words to respond but the only thing that came out was an unintelligible stutter. "B-b-b-but…"

He led me to the barn and sat in an old wicker chair that was propping open the door.

"I'm going to tell you a secret and I hope you can keep it. Can you promise?"

"Yes." I whispered.

"I have a way of knowing things about people who died. Sometimes they don't move on and I can feel them. When I sleep, they tell me their story, if they want to."

I wasn't sure what to say to him. I stared at him as if I had misheard. He smiled at me although it was as grim as his frown.

After a few seconds of silence he stopped smiling. "I know you will keep it a secret."

He rose from the creaking chair and strolled to his horse. It had been standing nearby unrestrained. My voice returned to me suddenly and I blurted the words before I realized I had spoken. "Can you find out who killed them and why?"

"In two days." He tipped his hat towards me and then mounted his horse.

A strong gust of wind blew me off balance as his horse kicked the dirt. Dust flew around me. I covered my eyes until the wind settled. The stranger was nowhere to be seen. Not a hoof print could be found.

I ran to the top of the hill by the burned house. From that height I could see for a couple miles in every direction but it was as if he had vanished. There were no dust clouds trailing beyond the hills.

Could it really be true? Could he really learn from the dead? Did he hear their voices? I hoped he would find that man from the barn and kill him. I wanted him to die, even if it made me a sinner.

Guilt eased across my thoughts and I abandoned them quickly and asked God for forgiveness. I watched birds nesting in the burned skeleton of Gray's house and listened for the sound of my friend's voice. I would do almost anything to laugh and play as we did a few days ago.

There was no sign of Pa or the ranger as I ran home. I could smell the beef stew Ma was cooking before I stepped onto the porch. The pain in my stomach reminded me that I had not eaten since morning.

I ate as fast as I could and then had another bowl. Afterwards, I helped Ma clean the table and wash the dishes. I did not mind helping because I needed a break from my thoughts.

"Can I sit outside tonight, Ma?" I asked once the last spoon was dried. The sun had set and Pa was busy cleaning his old shotgun at the table. I was rarely allowed outside at night when Pa was not there with me. She smiled and patted my head. I did not wait for her to change her mind and ran outside.

I sat in Pa's chair and listened to crickets and distant coyote howls. The tension in my back and shoulders eased. The wind grew stronger and several oak trees swayed and creaked as if they were dancing with the breeze.

The stars twinkled and I realized that no matter what happens, the world does not stop for anyone. Wisps of cloud passed by the moon as the breeze blew several dead leaves and some dust into a little whirlwind for a few seconds before collapsing. It was a beautiful night.

Staring at the stars and trees, I lost track of time. I stood, stretched my back, then walked to the edge of the steps to see the hills that hid Gray's house from view. I barely glimpsed the top of the hill when a cold wind slammed into me.

I teetered back a step and then leaned into the strange cold wind. A black shadow slid across the hills towards me. Thick dark clouds rolled across the sky till the night was pitch-black. The moon had been smothered and my hands were hardly visible.

Stumbling down the steps and into the yard, I stared at the darkness above. The sky filled with webs of lightning bolts spreading across the clouds and some towards the ground. A nice rain would do the crops some good. All thoughts of Gray were set aside as I ran inside to get some sleep. I needed to keep my strength up. A good rain meant we could get a strong crop this season. Pa will want me to be ready to work.

The next morning I awoke to my mother's call but I did not stir until the smell of cooking wafted across my nose. Bacon, eggs, ham, and hot biscuits made my mouth water as I washed and dressed.

"Good morning Ma." I said as I walked into the kitchen. She gave me a tiny smile as she piled up my plate.

I turned to the table to take my seat next to the ranger. He was looking at me from the corner of his eye but his head was turned to Pa at the head of the table. They seemed to be in deep conversation and Pa had not noticed me.

"I searched the house, but whatever caused the fire was probably burned up with everything else." The ranger explained to Pa.

"You think you can find out who caused the fire?" Pa asked before he saw me and nodded to the ranger which I knew meant to be silent. "Would you like a second helping, sir?"

"No thank you, I will probably have to loosen my belt already. This was the best breakfast I've eaten in many months."

"I was very happy to fix breakfast for someone other than these two silly boys." Ma replied with a slight smile.

As I dove into my breakfast, Pa and the ranger stepped out the kitchen door to the back of the house. The ranger was explaining something to Pa. Then Pa allowed a hesitant smile.

They walked back through the house and onto the front porch. Pa stood in the doorway as the ranger climbed onto his horse. "Don't worry, I'll find who did this to the Sandersons." I could hear him tell Pa.

Pa turned to me as the sound of hooves quickly drifted away. We smiled at each other. "Hurry and finish your breakfast, son. I need you to help me mend the fence Nugget knocked down last night."

"Again Pa? We ever gonna get a fence that the bull can't knock down?"

Pa shook his head and went out to the porch. "We might, if we get a good crop this year." He replied before the door closed.

The hours zip by when there is work to be done on the farm. I took off my shirt and used it to wipe the sweat from my head and wished some of the clouds from last night had lingered. As the sun rose over my head, my empty stomach complained.

Ma joined us with lunch as the last nail was hammered into the fence. She had timed it perfectly. We found a tree and sat under it while we enjoyed the fried chicken.

"Son, no matter what happens to me or your mother, we will always love you." Pa said as he ruffled my hair.

"It's not up to us when it's our time to go but our time will come. We will love you always. Grayson's was cut short but he did care for you the way friends often do. Just be happy with what you two did have with each other."

A lump formed in my throat and I felt as if I was going to choke on it. I stared at my breaded meat as a small tear formed in my eye.

"Pa? Will that ranger be able to find who did this to the Sandersons?"

He looked me straight in the eye. "Justice will come."

We finished eating and spent the rest of the day together working on various tasks. I knew my Pa was trying to keep me busy so I would not think about Gray. I did not mind helping so I was not upset about not playing that day. Playing would have reminded me that I missed him.

That night, Ma insisted that I take a warm bath to loosen up. Afterwards, the moment my head hit the pillow, I was asleep.

"Come on Gray! Keep up!"

I ran as fast and hard as I could and I knew Gray was catching me. I pushed myself harder to stay ahead of him. Glancing back, I found him standing on the last hill we had topped. Unsure what was wrong, I stopped and waved to him.

"Hey don't give up and then one day you'll beat me."

"Don't forget me." He replied with a sad smile and returned the wave.

"What do you mean? We're almost home. Don't stop now."

Gray smiled but his eyes seemed droopy and sad as if he was only smiling to reassure me.

Slowly he turned and walked from me. I ran after him but I could not get any closer to the hill. I pushed myself harder but despite my efforts the hill seemed to stay the same distance from me. I do not understand how I knew, but I did. If Gray escaped, I would never see him again.

"No, Gray. Come back. Come back! We are almost home! I promise to let you win if you come back. Don't leave me! Please, come back."

Gray disappeared down the other side of the hill and I was no closer to reaching it than I was when I had begun.

The sound of the rooster crow startled me awake. My eyes swelled and leaked tears. After a few minutes of wetting my shirt with tears and snot, I slipped out of bed. I washed up in the basin that I had poured water in the night before.

In the kitchen, Ma was sorting scrambled eggs and some potatoes onto plates for breakfast. "Are you okay?" She asked as she turned to me.

I could hear in her tone that she already knew the answer. "I miss Gray." I blurted.

She kissed my forehead. "I know, now sit down at the table and eat breakfast before it gets cold." The warmth of her lips on my head seemed to calm me a little but my spirits did not rise until the first bite slid into my belly.

As I chewed on a potato, I wondered if I had time to go to the creek and talk to Gray. Popping the last potato in my mouth and handing the plate to Ma, the front door slammed shut. Pa stormed in and grabbed my shoulder. "Son, I need you to go into town and pick up an axe handle. I forgot to get it yesterday."

"Yes, sir."

My heart leaped at the chance to go. Pa always let me keep the change to buy some candy when he sent me on errands like these. I ran to put on my shoes and met him on the porch.

He handed me a couple dollars "Stay away from that ranger if you see him."

"Yes, sir!" I ran as fast as I could. My cheeks ached from the huge grin that was stuck to my face. I could not shake the happiness at the thought of all the candy I was going to buy at the general store for Gray and me.

I arrived at the store and hesitated as I remembered there was no more Gray. It felt as if someone had hit me in the chest with a sledge hammer. I shook off the feeling and went inside before I embarrassed myself with tears.

I found the axe handle quickly but I was not in the mood for candy. It did not seem to be as much fun without Gray to share it with.

As I left the store, I saw the ranger sitting in a chair on the porch in front. "Someone told me to get this for you." He said to me. A green lollipop was lying in his palm.

Only Gray knew that green was my favorite color and only I knew his was red. That was one of our many secrets. I took the candy and examined it.

"Thank you, sir." I started to turn but my jaw started flapping. "How are you gonna find out who did it?"

He squinted at me. "Don't worry. I won't have to. They'll come to me. They always do and I can feel them nearby."

I nodded as if this was an acceptable answer and started for the street. He grabbed my shirt and pulled me behind him. His attention was down the street. Determination took over his features as the hand not pulling me against the wall of the store moved to rest on the revolver at his hip.

Shots fired in the direction the ranger was staring. Two men were galloping through town firing their guns at horses and people. They were at a full speed as they passed the ranger and me.

One of the men turned towards us with his pistol aimed but then his eyes went wide and he lowered the gun. The ranger was a blur as he drew his gun. The man's hat flew off his head before I realized the ranger had fired.

The man gasped and kicked his horse to speed up. He was the red eyed man in the Sanderson's barn. The villain raced his horse out of town after his partner. Their eyes were wide and their mouths hung over their shoulders as the ranger jumped off the walkway and landed on his horse.

He chased after them twice as fast as any horse I had ever seen. Wind and dust flew into the air behind him as he raced after the two men.

I chased after the ranger until the rising dust was no longer visible. Then I used a trick to follow the hoof marks that my Pa taught me while hunting deer. The ranger's horse left no hoof marks but the outlaws' horses were unmistakable.

The shadows from the fast moving clouds ran all along the ground and provided sporadic shade as the sun rose into the noonday sky. The trees whistled as they swayed in the wind.

The sound was almost comforting as it reminded me of an adventure with Gray last summer. That day we learned not to piss on rocks before checking for skunks sleeping under them. After Gray got sprayed he lost a tooth running into a low branch. We had been listening to the trees speak through the wind before watering the skunk.

Following the tracks into the woods, two miles from town, is where the shadows had stretched long on the ground. The sun was no longer as helpful as it lowered behind the trees. My mind had been on Gray and tracking the horses so much I had not realized the day had almost gone by. Pa will be angry that I had forgotten to bring home the axe handle which I must have left outside the general store.

The tracks led me to a place in the woods that Gray and I called the Devil's Chair. We had been hunting rabbits when we came upon a massive ugly old tree. The tree had been hit by lightning years ago. Burn marks still webbed across one side of its bark. It was bent and broken and looked like a giant chair. The biggest piece of trunk leaned on the ground with branches protruding along its width as if a gnarled hand was reaching to the sky. The top was smooth and looked like a giant seat with the branches circling it.

Beyond the chair shaped tree, two gunshots echoed. I recognized the deep throated laughter that followed. I ran on my tip toes to where I heard the shots, trying to make as little sound as I could. Lying next to a cactus was the ranger with an arm over his chest. He looked asleep. His hat was on the ground a few feet from him and beside it was the stranger that was with the man with the red eyes in town. The man was pale and stared at the sky with unseeing eyes.

I ran to the ranger to find that he was not breathing. Fear coursed through my veins as I saw any chance of justice slip away. I had no tears left after tracking the horses for so many miles in this heat.

I knelt beside him. "Wake up you can't be dead, you gotta be all right!"

Memories of Gray flashed in my mind and almost hurled me into a state of panic. The ranger was my only hope to catch those murderers. I needed him to live.

"I will be alright as soon as I stop bleeding." His voice grumbled.

The ranger was breathing again and staring at me. My mouth hung open and my eyes were so wide I thought my eyeballs would fall out.

"I thought you were dead."

"I can die, just not that easily." He offered me a hand. "Help me up and then go home!"

I pulled him up using every ounce of muscle I could. Then I lied. "I'll go home." I had no plans for that and he will be too busy to make sure I do.

His horse emerged from the trees after a short whistle from the ranger. He grabbed his hat and jammed it on his head without brushing it off.

He climbed onto his horse and rode so fast it seemed as if the horse was running on the wind. Maybe that was why I could not find any tracks.

The outlaws' horse tracks were still easy enough to follow. The sun was down and shadows were getting deeper as the sky filled with clouds. Everything was dark and quiet. If not for the constant lightning bolts threading across the sky I would have been blind. The tracks led me all the way to the edge of town.

The flashing weather illuminated the town well enough to catch glimpses of the buildings.

I heard gunshots and I noticed an orange glow coming from the middle of town. I headed that way and gasped as I saw the saloon engulfed in flames. Someone was shooting from inside. I ran to the store across from the saloon to find help but there was nobody around. It was as if everyone was hiding.

I stepped as close as I dared to the burning building where the ranger's horse was standing. I should not have been so close to the fire or these men but I had to discover what was happening inside.

A chair crashed through a window near me and clattered into the road as a man followed and rolled to a stop beside me. His eyes were filled with hatred, dark and empty. As his gaze fell on me his eyes burned with a red glow.

Red Eyes grabbed me by the collar and hit me. I fell to the ground with flashes of bright lights shining in my vision. When my sight cleared a little, he was aiming his gun at me and smiling. His teeth were broken and bloody.

"Stay still you mangy dog. You're the one who called him on us." His voice was hoarse, cracked, and full of menace. I heard the click of the hammer as he pulled the trigger then I heard it again but his gun never fired. His eyebrows creased together and he lifted the gun to find the problem when a big shape burst out of the broken window, knocking him to the ground.

It took a second for me to realize the ranger tackled him. I took a step back as the wind roared through the muddy streets.

I heard the voice of the villain rising from the fresh mud. It sounded dark and steady as he squatted, ready to pounce. "I know about you ranger. I'm not scared of you."

"Then stop running and let's get this over with."

He charged at the ranger and they traded punches. Each blow was in a strange rhythm that matched the lightning flashes above.

Rain suddenly poured so heavy that my vision was obscured. I ran behind a rocking chair and watched.

The ranger shoved him and shouted over the storm. "It's time you meet a friend of mine."

"We already met." Red Eyes retorted.

He slugged the ranger on the left eye, knocking him backward. The ranger stumbled and fell.

I was expecting the villain to jump on him but instead he ran into the general store. I climbed to the window and peeked in as the ranger pulled himself out of the mud and chased after.

The bad man grabbed a handful of bullets from behind the counter and loaded a couple into the gun as the ranger charged towards him. He pointed the gun as they were within arm's length of each other and the ranger skidded to a stop.

He was speaking but I could not understand him as the ranger backed out of the building and onto the edge of the porch. I sat under the window too afraid to move. Red Eyes stepped out of the door and finished his speech.

"…and I'm going to burn the rest of this town once you're gone."

His finger tensed and pulled when two loud bangs erupted. I covered my ears as I realized that it was not Red Eye's gun that had fired. Someone was behind me.

The stranger was sprawled on the porch with his feet towards me and struggling to breathe. From the shadows behind me came a rifle and then a woman I recognized. Ma stared down at the fallen outlaw.

"When it comes to my family, don't mess with 'em!"

The ranger watched Ma for a moment and then took off his hat as he stood over the fallen. It was at that moment I realized the outlaw had stopped breathing and lay as still as a stone.

"God have mercy on your soul because I won't." I heard the ranger's deep voice clearly in the pouring rain and thunder.

He then leaned down and covered the stranger's face with his hat. A horrible scream erupted. The body remained motionless, but the agonized terror that poured from the hat was very much alive. It must have been the stranger's soul that had howled. There was no other explanation for it.

I jumped to my feet and turned from the sounds. I wrapped my arms around Ma while tears mixed with the rainwater that escaped my hair.

I looked into her eyes. "How did you get here?"

"Pa fell off the horse and broke his leg while he was looking for you. So I brought him on over to doc's office when I heard gun shots."

I glanced to where the ranger was standing as the howling finally stopped and was jarred to find that the outlaw was no longer in sight. There was not a drop of blood on the wood where he had died. My head turned in every direction and I wondered if I had been imagining things.

Ma patted my shoulder gently. "Let's go see pa at doc's office."

I felt the tension welling inside of me deflate a little at the sound of her calm voice. I followed her to the Doc's office.

When we walked in, I saw Pa sitting on a table as the Doc examined his leg and was fitting together a splint to straighten it.

"I'm sorry, Pa."

"As long as your ma and me are alive, we will always look after you. Here." He held out a black handkerchief wrapped around something. As I took it, Pa continued. "The Ranger left this for you. He said that Gray wanted you to have this."

Whatever was inside was heavy. I carefully unraveled it and found two gold nuggets bigger than my fists.

I had not realized I left my mouth open till I took a breath and the sharp air stung my throat.

"He said this was meant for you to get a better life so that you could help others someday."

~~~~~~~~~~~~~~~~~~~~~~~~

Scratching my wrinkled nose, I wrap up the story as all the cadets stare at me. Some had their eyebrows raised in confusion or disbelief but a few looked at me as if I had told them they were going to go to the moon without a shuttle.

"I used one nugget to pay for the funeral for Gray and his parents and then bought their land. I built a new home there and made it a place for the less fortunate to stay until they could get on their feet. I called it Gray's Home."

Glancing around I notice the eyebrows dropping as they anticipate I am nearly done with my story.

I let out a tired sigh before I continue. "The other nugget I used to get a college education and become a Texas Ranger. As for the Broken Star Ranger, I heard rumors from far away of a man that fit the same description. They all said the same thing. He would help those in trouble that no one else could."

Some of the cadets glance at each other as I close my speech.

"Now, to all you rookies, it doesn't matter if you believe my story or not. One day you will have your own tale so I hope you will be here to pass on a piece of your history to another generation of Texas Rangers." I hesitated to let the words of what I said sink into their young minds. "We chose this profession to help those that need it so get out there and do what you chose to do."

I fell silent and grinned at all the young smiles around me. They may not believe my story but they do respect me for all the years of service. The class stands and salutes. My gaze drifts across them. All so young and I know some will never reach my age. Those that do will come to understand the point of my tale.

My heart swells with pride and admiration for the most honorary gesture I could think of. Clicking the locks on my wheelchair in place, I lean forward till all of my weight is on my legs. With all my might, I force myself to stand and return the salute with perfect posture.

~~~~~~~~~~~~~~~~~~~~~~~

Three months later retired Texas Ranger Captain Jacob Baker died in his sleep. On his head stone the words are written "Jacob liked the green lollipops, Gray liked the red ones." At the funeral over a hundred Texas Rangers from all over the state came and placed green and red lollipops upon his grave.

As the procession ended and everyone walked to their cars, a tall man with a black cowboy hat and a pink scar between his eyes emerged from the nearby trees and tossed a green lollipop into the grave.

"Say hello to Gray for me."

My Cave

A cave in my mind is where I live. It's a place where I can live without fear and bury my dreams in a shallow grave, where they can sleep. I don't care if my eyes can see; it is my mind that plays at night. The cave is what protects my monster from the world and I keep my monster with me inside and put away the hurtful words that the world screams at it. My monster cries at the words, the ugly words that the world screams at him. In the cave, I protect my monster from getting hurt, hope the world will forgive me, and let me sleep. I sit on the edge of a memory that haunts me when I sleep and it happens when life wants to play in my sleep. Neither madness nor happiness can be measured by the same ruler but nearly always gives the same answer, so drink with your mind the thoughts of happiness and remember to save some for later. Life may be plentiful but it is shallow so savor it for this moment. Now is the time to rest your weary head of all thoughts and watch as the clouds turn those thoughts into rain. Rain is a thing that must fall if we want it to or not but it is up to us how much we drink. This is the thing that we all need, so close your eyes, dream.

THE RIVER AND MY MADNESS: PART 1

I, Jacob Monroe, have seen horrible images that I do not understand. I do not have time to try and explain these sins that leave a burning taste in my mouth. Greed has destroyed my life. I do not blame my father for what he did but I do blame him for dragging me down with him. I pray sometimes that the Lord Almighty would forgive me of my sins.

In a moment of weakness I condemned my soul to walk the path of the damned forever. I am writing this in the hopes that whoever finds this will bring it to my sister, Victoria Monroe. She lives on the family farm which she worked hard to save from the banks after Ma and Pa died from a plague. I often dream of my childhood when I watched them die slowly. I felt so helpless.

I do not know how much longer I have to live. She is the only kin I have left besides my son David. I have never met my son and I do not know where his mother has taken him but Victoria knows. She needs to bring this journal to him so that he can save himself and resist the demon. Its temptations will drag him down to the same hell I am living in. Our family is cursed. Our souls are drained a little bit with every committed sin.

Victoria did not approve of my quitting school early to run out west and find my fortune in gold. She was courted by the son of a store owner named Daniel but I haven't seen her in two years. I was following my dreams until a few moments ago…

~~~~~~~~~~~~~~~~~~~~~~~~~

My stomach was full of the fish I had caught in the river that day. I had laid my bedroll close to the fire to keep away the critters. The fire did little to soften the freezing bite of the wind but I had enough whiskey in me to keep warm.

I stared into the stars and found the big dipper, dreaming of someday finding gold in these rivers. A star shot across the constellation and I closed my eyes and made a wish. After I was done, I kept them closed and listened to the sounds.

The crickets played high pitched music and frogs sang along. Wind whistled a sad tune through the weeds near the river. Small trickling sounds drifted from the water as it rolled over stones and against the banks. The noise was like a sweet lullaby that was slowly sending me to sleep.

Laying there, a cool breeze brushed past me and then the feeling of fingertips lightly touched my cheek. The fingers were colder than the winter air and for a moment I thought snow had fallen. I opened my eyes and kneeling beside me was a blond woman crying in silence.

I rolled to my feet in one swift motion. My boots were flat on the ground and I was pointing both pistols at her. I thought I was dreaming so I blinked and shook my head to wake up. The woman was gone. There was no sound nor an imprint in the dirt where she had been kneeling. It was as if she had never been there.

"What the hell? Damn that whiskey."

I stepped toward the spot I had been laying and put my guns in their holsters. I saw the imprint and scuff marks in the dirt where I had been sleeping but there was no sign of anyone else.

Something cold brushed against my shoulder. I turned and placed my hands on my guns but froze when I saw the woman again. My heart hammered in my chest. She stood before me but there were no tracks behind her as if she had appeared out of thin air.

She leaned towards me with quivering lips and whispered. "Save yourself."

I tried to ask her who she was but only mumbling sounds came from my mouth. I could see the river bank and the silhouettes of the trees through her. She kneeled to the ground and sobbed into her hands. Long platinum hair fell over her eyes and my heart ached for her.

I took my hands off my guns and kneeled beside her. I tried to comfort her although I did not know what I could do for a ghost. As my hand passed into her shoulder she turned to me. Her eyes had sunken into her head to leave two empty holes.

I felt the blood drain from my face and the air grew cold enough that my breath was visible. I tried to step back but I tripped over my feet and fell on my rear.

"Save yourself." Her voice was hollow and sad. "Help me, save yourself."

She walked to the edge of the river and stared at the water for a moment. I remained sitting on the ground and watched her. My pulse was slowing.

She turned towards me and in an instant flew at me with her hand outstretched. I tried to scream but there was no chance for sound to escape. The moment her fingertips touched my face I felt calmness pass through me and my body stiffened as ice then flowed into my veins.

She moved closer and rested her palm against my forehead. Images flittered in my mind and then everything was black.

I was in a dark room with a pile of bones on the stone floor. My heart should have pumped faster but I could not feel it. In fact, I could not breathe. I tried to get up but my body did not move. My legs were sprawled in front of me and I was leaning against a hard cold rock. Headless skeletons were scattered all along the walls. Flies buzzed across the remains, attracted to the smell of decay.

There was no sign of the ghostly woman by the river. My campfire had been replaced by the sound of buzzing flies and cold damp air. The cavern was illuminated by a reddish glow. I could not tell where it was coming from but it was everywhere. I tried to cry for help but my mouth sagged open and spittle ran down my chin.

The cry had caught in my throat as I looked across the stony floor of a huge cavern and saw a huge mound of skulls piled neatly in the center. The skulls looked mostly human but there were several that belonged to strange beasts I had never seen before and could not imagine what they were. Some were squat and horned, others long and narrow.

At the top of the mound, the skulls formed a throne and a figure shrouded in darkness was seated straight backed and unmoving. A soft orange flame burned on a red candle floating over the throne. The angle of the candle left the face in shadows but there was enough light to see that the silhouette was humanoid. The darkness that surrounded the body seemed to extend from it and obscure the tip of the mound where it sat.

Swarms of fat flies swirled in clouds around the figure. Sometimes the swarms would fly into its darkness and then fly out a moment later. The figure remained motionless, staring at the floor as if it was waiting or maybe it was as dead as the bones surrounding it.

"Where are you? You foul piece of shit!" A southern woman's voice, filled with rage, rang through the cavernous room. "I'm here to destroy you for all my kinfolk! I'll stop you from claiming any more innocent lives!"

She approached the skull throne from the edge of my vision. Chain armor hung from her shoulders to her knees. A leather cloak was draped across her shoulders and back.

Leather riding boots kicked dust into the air as she stormed towards the darkened figure. She brushed her long blond hair over a shoulder which then fell between her shoulder blades. A sword was held steady in its scabbard on her belt with her hand wrapped around the hilt.

The figure replied with an oily deep voice. "Innocent? You claim they were innocent but they were all born from sin. They are kin to the one that made the deal with me." His head tilted to the side and then he stood up. Towering several feet above the woman. "I savor the flavor of a soul that comes looking for me. The taste of anger is a delight I rarely get to enjoy anymore."

Sucking sounds came from the shadows and a long and forked tongue whipped the air around its head. The cheekbones puffed up in what could be a smile.

"Tell me your name little girl so that I can carve it into your skull before planting it in my throne." The dark voice echoed off the walls of the cavern and I realized it was not coming from the figure standing on the throne but from all around the cavern.

The woman drew the sword and charged the throne. "My name is Victoria!" She screeched at the monster.

The sword glowed golden as she ascended the pile of skulls. Every step higher up the mound, the deeper her legs dug into the pile, as if the skulls shifted to bury her deeper with every step. As she struggled to move on, the figure floated on the shadows and towards her. The red candle followed above the demon's head.

She stopped fighting the skulls that were swallowing her legs and waited for the figure to float within range of her golden blade. She swung so hard that as the blade passed through the shadowy form she lost her balance and rolled down the mound of skulls.

The figure continued to float over her without a scratch. Victoria tried to get to her feet as she landed on the stone floor but the figure was faster and grabbed her by the throat. She raised her sword but the shadows engulfed her arm and she screamed until she released the weapon. It clattered onto the floor and the glow winked out soon after. The shadows released her arm and swirled to hover behind the figure.

She tried to punch and kick the long arm holding her but her feet and fists dispersed it as if it was also made of shadow. It lifted her to its height and her feet dangled to the monster's knees. It leaned towards her but kept her fists out of range of its massive head.

Victoria gasped for air as she tried to claw at the fingers. After a few seconds she hung limp and he released her. She must have been barely alive because her breathing was shallow and slow.

The chest of the shadowy creature heaved as a cackling laugh rang through the cavern. Puffs of warm breath escaped the shadowed maw with every cackle. I tried to move but my body was dead. I had to find a way to stop this monster from killing her.

She stirred and moaned in pain. The creature stood over her and watched as she gasped for air, her hands rising to her throat. She climbed onto her knees and coughed. I was unable to do anything to help.

Her voice was raspy but she spoke with venom in her words. "You... should've... ki... killed me."

"My dear, Victoria. Do you think I would let you die so easily? How little you must think of your soul. You aren't angry enough to be tasty, yet."

She rose to her feet with her legs wobbling under her like a newborn foal. She rubbed her throat and shouted. "You will die, you piece of rotten shit from hell. I'll defeat you and free my brother's soul and all the other innocent souls you have taken."

"Innocent? Again with the innocent. Do you know what your brother did?"

Her attention was on the floor to search for her sword. The looming shadowy beast either did not notice or did not care.

"Victoria. I've been waiting many years for you to come to me and set him free. I've been waiting for you long before your brother came to me and begged for my services. After all that waiting, do you think I wasn't prepared for you?" Then I knew he did not care if she found the sword.

She spotted the sword partially hidden in the shadows by its feet. She lunged but the demon wrapped his fingers around her neck. It guided her to where she had fallen and held her.

"You're already dead, Victoria. I just haven't eaten your flesh yet. I want more anger or if you prefer, I think, despair tastes just as nice."

"Why don't you just kill me already?" Victoria remained fixated on the sword.

The creature's free hand waved away the hood of shadows and the candle tilted to illuminate its face. The nose and skin were burned to reveal a charred skull with muscle and tendon hanging from it. Blood oozed from the empty eye sockets and the fanged lipless mouth. He leaned forward till his breath blew her blond hair back and her attention turned on the demon.

"Now, do I have your undivided attention?"

Victoria paled but she had no other response. She had finally lost hope in defeating this thing.

"I'll take that as a yes. Before I eat your soul, let me tell you how patient I am. I have sat locked in this cavern for centuries. Many have come to defeat me for the glory of some Godly order or to simply sell their souls and make their dreams come true. The key to my escape has been to wait for two of the same kinfolk to willingly seek me out and sacrifice their delicious salty warm blood to me.

"You and your brother are going to set me free to dine on the sinned soaked souls that I have hungered for so long. My children have feasted on my flesh and those who never leave this place."

Flies swarmed in thicker clouds. The buzzing insects near me left their bones and joined the swelling buzzing mass that was filling the entire ceiling.

"Their countless numbers have become my children. They have spawned their maggots in my belly as I feasted upon them. These will be my spies, to find souls to feast on. They grow strong as they eat my flesh and crawl inside my body."

A light cackle escaped the monster and then he continued. "I am a never ending food supply that tickles me when they eat too much. They have become strong and now hunger for living flesh. Once I have regained my full strength from the souls of the wicked, I will go forth and devour the whole world. My children will eat everything."

Flies zipped from its eyes, nose, and mouth. Victoria struggled to escape as they swarmed over her. She screamed but flies crawled into her mouth and gagged her.

"They will lay eggs in your belly and the maggots will hatch and eat their way out. Oh don't worry, Victoria. When the eggs hatch, your skin will be devoured. Your body will live while they feast on your insides but you won't feel the pain anymore. Your soul will be bound to me and I will let you wander."

Victoria was weakening, her hands fell to her sides and her breathing almost stopped. The creature held her as she disappeared into the cloud of flies. A bloodied hand emerged from the massive living ball and grasped at the creatures arm, digging fingers into the smoky limb.

"Doesn't it feel so pleasurable at first? Thousands of tiny nibbles on your flesh then they dig deeper and deeper."

A gargled scream escaped the buzzing mass and several flies were dislodged but quickly returned to the frenzy. I tried to move but my body did not respond. I had to escape this place.

"Why are you here?"

I saw the empty eyes focusing on me and a bloody bony finger pointing towards me. He released Victoria and the flies swarmed into the air for a moment. I got a glimpse of a blood covered Victoria staring at me and mouthing. "Save yourself," and then the flies descended on her.

Victoria was buried under the swarm as the creature was already upon me, leaning towards me till its rotten nose was almost touching mine. I tried to move but I knew I was wasting my time. I squeezed my eyes shut, waiting to be torn apart or worse, eaten by flies.

But nothing happened.

I awakened as the eyeless ghost of Victoria pulled her hand from my forehead. I collapsed. I shivered with cold and my clothes stuck to my moist skin. My mouth felt as if it had been stuffed with cotton.

Victoria drifted away, crying in her hands. I tried to rise but I couldn't get off my elbows. Her feet entered the water on the bank and I could no longer hold myself up. I fell and stared at the stars. My muscles twitched as I tried to move them but they were becoming as numb as they had been in the dream.

The stars blurred and smeared as my eyes struggled to stay open. The sound of laughing in the woods surrounded me but I could not lift my head.

For a moment I thought sleep would overtake me but the feeling in my arms and legs began to return. My vision cleared but that loud cackling laughter continued as I rolled onto my hands and knees.

"Boy! I hope you haven't been waiting long for me." A deep voice thundered from the sky.

I had my guns in my hands and pointed them from my hips as I searched for the source of the unnatural voice. The laughing had stopped when the voice spoke but I never knew where it had been coming from. The ground seemed to bow and shift which made my feet unsteady. I tried to shake the dizziness as the back of my neck tingled.

I knew I was being watched.

I turned to the river as bubbles popped around the center. A dense white fog rolled from behind my legs and hid my feet. I felt the hair on my arms and legs rise as I knew that fog travels from a river, not towards it.

My feet felt frozen. The chill ran up my legs into my chest and my arms slowly lowered to my sides. I heard my pistols hit the dirt but I never felt them leave my hands. I realized then that I could not feel my hands. I felt compelled to turn so I did.

Thick cold fog rose over my head until I couldn't see anything past my nose. There was a pain in my chest as my heart hammered until I could not hear anything else but its rapid pounding beat.

A warm breeze blew the fog across me. I swore I heard a woman whisper. "Be strong, have faith." I remained frozen in place, afraid to trip.

Finally, the fog gave way. I was facing the forest with the river to my back. A giant door was hovering a few inches from the ground. It was wooden with a single hinge along one side and wrapped in barbed chains with rusted spikes as long as my fingers. In several places the spikes were embedded in the wood. There was no knob but on the opposite side of the hinge was an upside down keyhole.

Moisture beaded in my underarms as I stared at the strange chained portal. I did not know what the abominable thing was for but my heart raced at the sight of it. A sudden sense of dread overwhelmed me and tears formed in my eyes. There was no point in going on with my life, no point to life at all.

I wiped at the tears and mumbled. "Lord, please…"

The chains rattled along with the cackling. The laughing lasted for a few seconds and then a voice spoke. Like the laugh, it sounded almost muffled.

"Are you afraid?"

Still mumbling I said. "N… n… no."

The chains rattled with every syllable. "Well that's good. Scared people run and I want you to stay and play. After play time is over, I will feast on your flesh and swallow your soul."

After a few seconds of silence, the chains glowed and steamed. I felt the heat through my clothes as the links drooped. The metal turned white and I had to avert my eyes for fear of burning that light into my vision. The chains slipped from the frame as they stretched and liquefied. They sizzled in the dirt as the molten metal burned evaporated. I wondered if they left marks on the ground but the full moon was not bright enough to see once the fires had gone out.

The wood grain pattern began to shift. It was slight but the moonlight shining on it allowed me to see it clearly. The grain twisted until it outlined a wicked face with horns and fangs surrounded with flames. It smiled as smoke billowed from the doorjamb.

Flames crept from the image and the edges of the frame ignited. I felt hypnotized as my gaze locked onto the fire climbing along the doorway and then across it. Then something slammed into the other side. The noise was so loud that I broke from my trance and fell on my rear.

I trembled as it banged again and again. On the third knock the door cracked and splintered, after the fourth it bowed towards me, on the fifth it exploded.

My head hit the dirt as shards of wood zipped past me, some igniting in midair. Everything seemed to move in slow motion as my mind tried to register what was happening. The explosion left my ears ringing so I could not hear the pieces showering into the dirt, rocks, and river. I could only hear the sound of my heart pounding in my chest and my panicked breathing.

Flaming fragments bounced around me. I did not feel the burn when an ember bounced off my leg. I could not believe this was happening. I could not hear or feel anything so maybe I was dreaming.

A large burning chunk of wood fell from the sky. I saw it coming but I could not move as it struck me in the head. Everything went black immediately but there was no pain.

I do not know how long I was unconscious but the moon was in the sky and my fire was burning low. I sat up, holding my head. There was a knot on my forehead but there was more pressure than pain.

The frame was hanging in the air but the door itself was scattered in smoking bits. I expected to see the woods through the frame but instead there was nothing.

The darkness inside swirled like a pool of oil devouring the light from the moon and my campfire, the frame hummed and creaked. Then came heavy steps that vibrated the ground beneath me. I knew whatever was coming for me was going to kill me. I closed my eyes and hoped that I had been a good enough person that God would receive my soul.

"Ssssleeeeeep." A deep voice bellowed out of the open portal.

And so I did.

I Am Nobody

I am nobody.
I am hated loathed ridiculed and laughed at for being what I am.
I am nobody.
I am nobody, am not a hero
I am nobody.
I am no one famous.
I am nobody.
I am not of any importance.
I am no one
I am the "nobody" that held open the door for you when you needed an extra hand and didn't say thank you.
I am nobody.
I am the "nobody" you bumped in the hallway making me spill my coffee and didn't say sorry.
I am nobody.
I am the "nobody" that helped you pick up your paperwork that you dropped and didn't say thank you.
I am nobody.
You can now go on with your happy life and never be bothered by anybody again because "nobody" died today.

A GUNSLINGER WITH A CONSCIOUS

I was a gunfighter in my younger days. If somebody looked like they wanted trouble I gave them more than they could handle. I killed more men and horses than I can remember. I even killed a blind man's dog.

Back then, every kid with a gun tried to kill me. I had killed without an ounce of remorse. I was so fast that some thought the devil protected me and there was no reason to change what they believed. My reputation grew as did the bounty on my head. It must have been 100,000 pesos the last I heard.

I packed my rifle in the saddle as I prepared to ride off to a new town. It was a small hope that nobody would know me there but my reputation had spread farther than I had ever traveled and so had my wanted posters.

My black hat, raincoat, and boots usually gave me away before anyone saw my pretty face. I needed to stop shaving so those posters were not so accurate.

"Hey Cowboy." The voice of a young woman sounded off behind me. I did not recognize her voice but I was pretty drunk last night at the boarding house. I cannot remember the woman I slept with.

I spun around with a big stupid grin. Instead of a pretty

smile, the barrel of a revolver was wobbling in my face. The tiny young woman tried to hold it steady. She was obviously not comfortable with a gun but her finger was on the trigger. At this distance, she would not miss.

"You killed my husband."

"I've killed a few." I calculated the seconds it would take her to pull the trigger with those shaking hands and decided I might be able to shoot her first. She was pretty so I really did not want to.

"You killed him because he walked into your horse! He just tripped; he never meant to touch your stupid horse."

Now I wanted to shoot her. The worst thing to say to a man is calling his horse stupid. My hands were fast. I raised the gun to her chest and for a split second I thought I had her. She pulled the trigger and I felt metal hit me right between the eyes. My vision flashed and then went black but I could feel my hands. I pulled the trigger and heard the woman scream so I aimed a little higher and pulled the trigger again. Her scream cut off to confirm that she was no longer a threat.

Then I felt the ground on my back. I had not realized I was falling until the air rushed from my lungs. Am I dead? I could feel my limbs, the beat of my heart, and the desperate ragged breaths. Panicked and confused, I tried to make myself sit up as the light began to return but the pain in my head grew. I tried to rub it but that made it worse and my fingers came away warm and wet.

How am I not dead? She did not miss me. I felt the bullet. Maybe she packed the bullet wrong and it misfired. The misfire must have slowed the bullet enough to not penetrate my skull. I should be dead; I might have been if she had shot me in the eye. Fool woman must have loaded the gun herself.

The pain pounded along with the beat of my heart as if it was trying to burst free. If I did not leave then someone else would try to finish the job.

With the warm blood running from my eye and across

my nose and chin, I was finally able to see well enough with my left eye. I mounted my horse and I hugged his neck praying I did not lose too much blood before I could get far enough to be safe.

My horse carried me for a couple miles and stopped in a small clearing in the woods. I slipped off the horse with blood in my eyes and dripping from my nose. I used the last of my strength to pull my saddle bag off the horse. I dropped to my rear and stared at the bag, wondering why I was on the ground. Why was I holding my bags? What is all this warm wetness on my chest?

I moved to a broken log as my legs wobbled like they had no bones. I gulped two big swigs of whiskey and then poured a little less on a torn stained wash cloth. I placed the rag over my face and inhaled the fumes. My nostrils burned but I barely noticed as the fiery pain from the hole was spreading. My senses began to clear and everything that happened came crashing into my consciousness.

She may not have killed me but that woman sure as hell injured me more than any man ever had. The left eye was completely clear. My right eye was filled with silhouettes and shadows.

I sighed and leaned, completely relieved. "At least I won't be blind."

Tipping the bottle with my free hand, I let the last of the whiskey pour down my throat in hopes to numb the pain. Spying some leftover beef jerky in the sack, I ripped off a piece and then chewed it slowly. I needed strength before someone got brave and tracked me.

After a while, I tied the rag around my head and angled it over my brow. The wound was covered and soaking in the whiskey. The pain was numbed but I was exhausted.

I sat there on the log until the sun set. My eyes had become difficult to keep open. I longed to lie down and sleep but my mama used to say that when you had a head wound and slept, there was a chance you might not wake up.

I made a small fire from leaves and short branches to keep warm. There was an unusual chill in the air on this July evening. My hands were trembling but I refused to sit on them to make them stop.

A twig snapped behind me and I was on my feet with both guns drawn. I shouted, "Who's there?"

Out of the shadows of some nearby trees, someone stepped into the light of my fire. He had two pistols in his outstretched hands pointed right at my head.

"I heard you were in town. I'm surprised you're still standing. I figured it'd be easier to bring you in if you had been shot, old timer."

Light glinted off the star on his chest. He was young; crow's feet had not begun to form at the corners of his eyes. However, I did not underestimate his inexperience. He was physically in his prime. I steadied both my guns at his chest.

The boy ranger spit and sneered at me. His voice was calm and confident. "I can take you anytime. I'll be known as the ranger that shot you down."

The fool boy, if he had intended to take him, he missed his chance. We stared at each other for several seconds. The ranger must have been waiting for a signal from me. Did he want me to put down my guns and surrender? Maybe he was waiting for reinforcements. Whatever his reasoning was, I needed to get moving.

"If you don't turn around and leave, boy, your ranger friends are gonna find you dead tomorrow."

I could feel the weakness creeping through the temporary adrenaline induced strength. It took nearly all my concentration to stand there without tipping. I really did not feel up to killing a stupid kid at the moment. The fact that a woman put me in this situation was already bothering me. This kid ranger wants to take me in and make everyone think he is some kind of hero.

He shifted to take aim but I fired before he could pull his triggers. Both of my bullets punched him in the chest as his guns went off. I felt the wind rush by my ear as a bullet almost hit its mark.

He dropped onto his back and fired off another couple rounds but none were close to me.

I lowered my revolvers as I watched the final rise and fall of his chest.

"I think you'll be known as the ranger who missed." Fool kid.

Pain shot up my legs as I crashed to my knees. It felt like I was falling but I couldn't be sure as everything went black. The pain was gone as soon as I hit the ground.

I awoke to an old brown skinned man kneeling beside me. Animal skins were laced together to create a canopy that surrounded us. I had never seen the inside of a teepee before.

Why was I here? I tried to get up as he spoke to me but I could not understand the words. My skull pulsated as if someone was pounding inside my head with a hammer. Each pulse held me tighter to the floor.

He leaned over me and I realized he was not as old as I first suspected. The wrinkles were not deep in his leathery brown skin and his eyes were clear. Life was hard for him and his people.

There were two knife cuts across his chest and three healed bullet holes on the arm closest to me. There was a horrible scar across a shoulder that looked like it could have been a bear bite. His long black hair was tied back and his eyes were strained in concentration as he continued a chant of some kind. He must have been a shaman or medicine man.

He took a black leather pouch from his hide belt and poured some black powder into one of his hands. After tossing some on the floor, a swirl of smoke formed and then a small fire was burning where the black powder fell. The sudden blaze made my skin crawl. Was this a nightmare?

The shaman threw black powder on the fire creating thick dark colored smoke. The smoke filled the tepee and then faded. He stopped chanting as the fire died. The breeze outside and the crickets became silent.

Where the fire had been was a drawing in the sand. It was a cowboy with a long coat and a four point star drawn across his chest.

He pointed at the design. "The Great Wolf Spirit came to me in a dream and told me that one day I would find a dying man with a hole in his head beneath a full moon. He will be a bad man but he will have a chance to undo his evil by helping others."

He poured some black powder on my wound and I felt the skin tighten. I did not have the strength yet to stop him as he removed the old cloth I had wrapped. I rubbed my fingers across the rough bump on my head and felt a dimple like scar.

"The scar will always be there so that you can never forget what you have done. Your soul is protected and your life will be long."

"Long life? I doubt that." I croaked.

"The Great Wolf Spirit said you have a lot to answer for. You will not pass onto the next life until you have paid your price."

I grunted at him, unsure as to what he was saying. I briefly wondered where my revolvers were. Would I have to kill this shaman to escape?

A light flashed and when my vision cleared I saw the woman holding the gun to my head. Tears streamed from her red and swollen eyes. The pain I caused her sparked a flicker of guilt in my heart and I struggled to push away the emotion. Then she was gone.

I stared at him while he sat patiently. He nodded as if he was aware I had drifted off but was paying attention now.

"My name is Little Tree and I am on a shaman's quest in the spirit world where I felt the sorrow of a boy. You must journey into that world and find your spirit guide."

The chanting began as he threw black powder on me. I closed my eyes and heard whispering voices call my name. Their painful cries for justice were venomous and angry. They grew louder until my ears ached. I shouted for them to stop and covered my ears but the voices would not be muffled.

They wanted justice for their pain. Their rage for the ones that caused their early departure from life was overwhelming. I screamed for them to be quiet as each one buzzed with frenzy. Every voice pounded in my head like another bullet between my eyes.

Then I felt small hands grab my wrists. The voices and the pain faded and I felt calm. I peeked to find a young boy standing in front of me. I lowered my hands and his hands shifted to continue covering my ears. A soft glow seemed to emanate from his body. The light split upward into the shape of a pair of white wings.

He smiled. "You must help me find my friend." He whispered.

The tepee and the shaman were gone. A soft glow of light that came from everywhere surrounded me. I was not sitting on anything, just floating in the light.

"Where are we?"

"We are in the between, a place where those who are murdered are to wait."

"What are they waiting for?"

"To be called into Heaven." The boy then frowned as he continued. "But those who are murdered have to wait for the ones that killed them so that they can be a witness when their murderers are judged. Some have been waiting for a long while. Sometimes the cries of the innocent have gone unheard for far too long. That's why you are here. You are to be the one who will bring justice faster. You will send the murderers into the between so there will finally be peace for their victims."

"How will I do that?" I pause to rub my chin. "I have

killed too many people myself. Wouldn't that mean I should be facing justice for my murders?"

"You will face justice in time but not until you get a chance to redeem yourself."

His little hands squeezed my ears and he pulled my head closer to him. He tilted my head so that he could put his mouth close to my ear. I tried to hold back but his strength surprised me. I was not sure I could have pulled away if I wanted to.

He whispered in my ear. "Always listen to Mother Earth, for she is wise and has been around a long time. She will provide you with everything you will need to survive."

"What about my spirit guide? Am I supposed to find an animal here?"

"The innocent will be your guide, the innocent that wait for rest."

I closed my eyes as he released me. I felt the ground on my back. When I opened my eyes I saw the interior of the teepee and the chanting old medicine man sitting beside me. I watched him until he stopped.

"You will travel with the knowledge that you will help the innocent find peace." He explained as he handed me the bag with the mysterious black powder. "This contains the tears of the innocent. You should pour a little on the bodies of those that you are sending to be judged."

I did not respond but took the bag and sat up. He raised his hands above his head. "It is time for me to finish my quest to the Half People who need my help."

He flicked his hand at me and I was enveloped by a bright light. I covered my eyes and glanced between my fingers. The light was blinding but there was no longer a teepee nor the shaman.

The sun was rising above the mountains. There was no pain in my head so I rose to my feet. There was no trace of the teepee or of any fire other than my own cold pile of ash, not even a sign of the young ranger I shot.

The sky was a bright blue and I was sweating. I found

my horse tied off on a mesquite tree next to where I had awakened. The saddles were packed with food and ammo. I did not remember getting any supplies.

Unsure of what happened the last few hours and what I was supposed to do, I decided to do what my mother would have done. I got on my knees. I placed the little black bag on the ground and said a quick prayer of thanks. I should be dead but somehow I was not.

The brightness of the morning sun was beginning to hurt my eyes. The relentless strain was causing a headache. I reached for the little black bag and instead found a black hat. If I was sure everything the night before was a dream I would have been shocked but by this point I was beginning to realize my life was no longer in my own hands. My old hat was nowhere to be found.

After I put the new hat on, I felt a poke inside my vest pocket. It was a Texas Ranger badge with the top point of the star ripped away. The badge of the ranger I had shot. I returned it to my pocket and climbed on my horse. There was no pain from the wound in my head as I rubbed my fingers across the scar. It would serve as a reminder to me for the remainder of my days. Whatever that meant, I did not know yet.

I was lost in my thoughts of the young ranger and the shaman who must have saved me. I could not piece it all together. It did not make sense to me why or how I am supposed to help people who were already dead.

The horse trotted across the grassy fields between the clumps of mesquite trees scattered across the hills. As the sun almost reached its peak in the sky, I saw a dust cloud traveling towards me along the road I was riding parallel to.

Turning my horse towards the cloud, I wanted to ask for directions from whatever stage coach that was barreling down the road.

I locked eyes with the driver of the wagon. They were filled with terror and his mouth was contorted as if he wanted to shout. Then I saw what was chasing him.

Behind the coach were two men with guns drawn and riding horses. They were closing in fast, trying to maneuver to get a clear shot at the driver.

I pulled the star out and stabbed the pin through my vest and drew a revolver. The two bandits glanced at me and turned their horses into the trees. I drew my second revolver and fired a shot from each gun. Both bandits fell from their horses and rolled along the ground.

As the stagecoach driver slowed to see what had happened, I dismounted my horse by the two fallen men. I stood over the first that had fallen. His shoulder was covered in blood but he would not die from that wound. His breath was slow and steady and his eyes were closed.

I am not sure why but I felt the urge to lay my hat on his face. As I did, he screamed. After a few seconds there was silence. When his chest stopped rising, I knew I had just sent my first soul to be judged.

The other outlaw was holding his stomach with bloody hands and trying to stop the life from flowing through the exit wound. His eyes were wide and his breaths were quick and short. He had seen everything that had happened to his partner.

He tried to run but he had already lost too much blood. He pitched onto his side groaning in agony. It was not hard to catch him. He lay there staring at me with pleading eyes.

"P… please don't kill me."

There was not enough strength left in him to struggle. I could not fight my destiny. His mouth opened to scream but nothing came. I felt no remorse as I lay the hat on his head. He did not scream like the other but released a whimper. When I removed the hat, his face was pale. His eyes were bloodshot and his mouth was twisted.

I was compelled to kneel and so I prayed over the dead. His sins must have been great to have suffered that much. The other bandit was not disfigured and appeared to be sleeping. "God, please forgive me for what I just done. Amen."

Any thoughts to extend the prayer left me as I heard the wheels of the stagecoach grinding towards me on the dirt road.

The driver pulled up and looked at the two dead men. He saw the badge on my vest and gave me a toothless smile. "Mighty thanks to you ranger. I thought they was going to get me for a minute there."

"They won't be getting anyone now."

The Driver looked at me and tilted his head. "Well, thank you again, sir. I'm going to tell everyone about the ranger with a broken star that saved me. What's your name?"

"Broken Star Ranger, that sounds like the perfect name." There were no wanted posters for that man.

Bottom Of My Cup

In the bottom of my cup I see my reflection and my reflection shows me a sad little nose, a sad little mouth, sad little eyes and a sad lonely little tear sliding down my face as my mind reflects in the bottom of my cup. In the corner of my cup a reflection of a sad little child sleeps there and that is all I see. My mind wanders in circles in silence as the child sleeps. My mind echoes my secrets in the bottom of my cup as the rest of my secrets slowly run down my face. Now on this hour I will wait because that is all I can do for my secrets to stop falling. Here in the bottom of my cup is where we are not afraid of being ourselves. Down here is where you can't hurt me anymore.

DO YOU BELIEVE IN GHOSTS?

My name is Victor Don Harris and I am a medical examiner for Harris County, in the Houston area. I have seen some strange things in my life but never anything as strange as the case I am sharing with you.

I did not know whether I could believe the stories the detective had told me and I admit after seeing the scene of the incident, I have no idea what to believe. I found the book mentioned in the report and could not help myself. I thumbed through it a few times, it did not seem to be anything remarkable but I was drawn to it. I found it in my pocket at the lab as I was drawing blood samples but I do not know how it got there.

It flooded my thoughts like some kind of drug obsession until I finally opened it and began reading. I am almost finished with it but that is a story for another time.

I have attached the autopsy report on the following pages.

==================================

Autopsy Summary Report

==================================

Reported Date: 2/29/04 Time: 04:37 Case: 04-011869 (001)
Code: INCIDENT   Crime: DEATH INVEST
Occurrence Date: 2/29/04   Day: Sunday   Time: 2:45-3:00
Location: 2700 South West Loop, Houston   RD: ST

==================================

Start time: 09:00   End time: 13:00

Autopsy performed by: Sr. M. E. Victor D Harris II

Notes: I, Sr. Medical Examiner, have performed the autopsy on Tim Dunn. Dunn was found dead in a Wellness Room at the State Psychiatric Mental Institution after being placed there for his own safety. I have come to the conclusion that Tim Dunn died due to severe blood loss from a six inch laceration just below his umbilicus.

From my examination at the scene of the incident, I noted the writing on the walls. The tales about voices and ghosts haunting Mr. Dunn was written in his own blood. Mr. Dunn cut himself with a large canine tooth of an unknown origin. He dipped the tooth in his blood and used it as ink. He eventually experienced syncope from the wound he had created but not before reattaching his restraints, including the straight jacket.

There was no sign of foul play outside of his self-inflicted wound. The doctors stated he had been dressed in a hospital gown when he was restrained. He had not been allowed to bring anything else with him and nothing else was found on his person during their initial search while restraining him in the bed.

The origin of the canine tooth is a complete mystery. The hospital staff claimed that they had not seen it before and that they would have secured it if they had.

My conclusion to this autopsy is that Mr. Dunn died due to loss of blood from a self-inflicted wound. I have no choice but to believe that the deceased had committed suicide.

Cause of Death: Suicide

Reason: Loss of blood due to a six inch laceration under the umbilicus.

Weapon: A tooth belonging to a large canine, possibly a wolf. The tooth has been sent to forensics which will determine its origin.

T.O.D.: approximately 2:45 to 3:00

==================================
Supplement Report
==================================
Reported Date: 2/29/04   Time: 04:37   Case: 04-011869 (001)
Code: INCIDENT   Crime: DEATH INVEST
Occurrence Date: 2/29/04   Day: Sunday   Time: 2:45-3:00
Location: 2700 South West Loop, Houston   RD: ST
=============NARRATIVE===========

On Sunday, 2/29/2004, at around 04:37 I, Detective John Alba, arrived on the scene. Hospital staff had discovered the body on a routine bed check a few minutes earlier. The medical examiner estimates the time of death between 02:45 and 03:00.

Tim Dunn was found deceased in his hospital bed. It appears that he used a canine tooth to cut into his lower abdomen and used the blood to write on the wall. The canine tooth was recovered from his left hand which was covered in his own blood.

I believe that somehow Dunn slipped out of his restraints sometime during a power outage. He then used the tooth to cut himself and use the blood as ink on the wall. Mr. Dunn had two hours to write his story and then return to his restraints before losing consciousness.

The power outage in the hospital affected this wing of the ward and the camera systems monitoring the area were disabled during the incident. Forensics has taken photographs of the entire room.

I was able to get two signed affidavits from witnesses who complained about a howling dog that sounded as if it was in the hallway an hour before the power outage. I believe this to be the source of the tooth but how it got into the wellness room and why there is no trace of the animal being there, I do not know. The forensics team has swept the scene for animal hair but so far has not reported any present.

===================================
Written Evidence
===================================
Reported Date: 2/29/04   Time: 04:37   Case: 04-011869   (001)
 Code: INCIDENT   Crime: DEATH INVEST
Occurrence Date: 2/29/04   Day: Sunday   Time: 2:45-3:00
Location: 2700 South West Loop, Houston   RD: ST
===================================

The following is what Mr. Dunn wrote on the wall:

In the mirror of my thoughts are the reflections of my past that I thought could not find me in the hour I buried them so I sang a happy little thought of a dream. I buried them deep in a graveyard with all of the rest of my happy thoughts.

In my soft white prison is where I write to you without the use of pencil, pen, or paper. My mind is wondrous and I have found a way.

Am I insane? Of course not because I am as sane as the man lying on the metal table in the next room. Enough of that because all I really want to know is do you believe in ghosts?

My friend Jacob did not, at least not until the night the doctors came and took him to the asylum. While we waited, he told me about a little letter he found in a book he was reading that same night.

It started one late evening when he was looking for a book on ghost haunting and paranormal activities. He was writing a research paper for a class. While he was in the college library, he turned down the aisle for paranormal research and discovered a book lying in the middle of the floor.

His curiosity got the better of him and he picked it up. On the cover in crimson red was written 'Welcome To My Imagination' and below the words was the drawing of a little boy who seemed pale. Jacob wasn't sure the book was what he was looking for but it intrigued him.

The small boy was a drawing of a semi-transparent ghost. He flipped through the pages and read a few random lines. It inspired him and he hoped that this book was exactly what he needed for his report.

His mind fell into a haze and he almost drove his car over a couple pedestrians and into several parked cars as his thoughts obsessed on the book. It almost felt as if he was in some sort of hypnotic trance.

When he got home, he rushed by the stack of other books he had purchased for his research paper and plopped on his old worn recliner. He stared at the cover as if nothing else existed.

The air dropped in temperature, after a few seconds of shifting and getting comfortable. So shocking was the cold, Jacob almost missed that the sounds from the streets below his dorm window had grown completely quiet. It was as if everyone had decided to go home all at once.

Trying to ignore the coolness that was raising goose bumps on his arms, he opened the book to the acknowledgments. As he read the first word, his phone rang. Jacob stared at it for a moment but did not answer. He always waited for a second ring in case it was a wrong number that would hang up before a second ring.

Just as he thought, there was no recurring ring so he returned his attention to the book. Again, as he read the first word the phone rang once more. There was no second ring and Jacob grunted and returned his attention to the book. Then it rang again. Jacob was getting frustrated and answered it without hesitation. After hearing the dial tone, he slammed the receiver and looked at the book. When the phone rang again, he grabbed it quickly.

"Who is this?"

He was answered by silence. There was no dial tone.

"Is this Larry or Orion? You guys better stop fucking with me. I'm trying to do some research."

He hung it up and sat to read when the phone rang again. Disgusted by his friend's humor, he yanked out the cord and threw it on the floor.

"Try prank calling now. That's not funny."

Without any further interruptions, Jacob finished the first chapter in a few minutes. He had always been a quick reader and his impatience to absorb the contents of the book pushed him to read faster.

As he turned to the second chapter and read, he heard someone calling him.

"Jacob."

Laying the book open so as not to lose his place, Jacob then rose from the chair. After listening for a moment he cracked the door and glanced into the empty hall.

Scratching his heat, he sat to read again.

"Jacob."

A growl rose from his throat and he kept the book while he checked the hall. There was nobody in sight. Other than a couple of guys he did not recognize at the end of the hall swapping girl stories, the hall was vacant.

He decided to stand in the open doorway to read and catch which of his friends is trying to harass him.

"Jacob."

Whipping his head back and forth, no nearby doors were ajar and a chill ran along his spine. He slammed the door. His frustration melded with his confusion and he grumbled to himself as he returned to the chair.

He flipped the book open, ignoring the voice calling his name.

"Jacob."

"Jacob."

He concentrated harder and realized this book was not going to be as much help as he thought. It was about some strange haunting but not a real investigation of a haunting as he had thought. He needed a serious book but he would continue reading anyway. It was too intriguing to stop.

He finished another chapter and craved more so he read on into chapter three. A soft cool breeze brushed across his face like fingers lightly rubbing his cheek. He held his breath. The hair on his arms and neck stood straight.

The reading lamp beside him flickered and then left him in a cold blanket of darkness. The shadows were broken by a sliver of moonlight on the floor in front his chair.

He fought the scream rising in his throat. He tried to steady his voice as he spoke.

"Those damn breakers are always going out!"

He stood and dropped the book on his left foot. The book flipped open next to the chair and a folded piece of paper fell into the moonlight.

The momentary fear of the dark passed as he focused on the paper and leaned to pick it up. Just as his fingers touched the paper, voices whispered from the corners.

Losing his nerve for a moment, Jacob fell on the floor and sat against the recliner. He squinted into the blackness as the shadows deepened.

Unable to see anything, he tried to ignore the whispers and stared at the paper. His jaw ached from clenching. He unfolded the paper, the only thing written was a few words sloppily scribbled in blue ink. They read: 'Do you believe in ghosts?'

A cold sensation flowed up his backside as he squatted on the floor in the moonlight. He turned to the boy from the cover standing over him. The boy stared at him with tears on his rounded eyes.

Jacob's scream woke the entire floor and we all ran into the hallway with a fearful and yet sick fascination that someone was getting murdered. The scream was terrifying and as I write this my blood turns cold.

I was the first to the door and found it locked. I kicked it open and flipped the light switch on. I crept into the doorway quietly. I was expecting to find blood everywhere.

Nobody followed me in but the doorway was crowded with spectators peering into the dorm. Everyone was as frightened to find a body as I was.

I found Jacob hiding behind his recliner with sweat glistening on his goose bump covered skin. I approached him carefully, not sure what to expect.

He handed me a book and then he told me everything that had happened to him. I then noticed that his skin had a pale sheen too it as if he had been drained of all color.

As the doctors came and took him, I read the paper sticking out of the book and I only have one question for you.

Do you believe in ghosts?

Tears Of My Truth

I do not cry because you said I am an ugly.
I do not cry because you laughed at me.
I do not cry at all the names you called me
I do know that everyone needs someone to make fun of, so I am here
to make you feel better. I don't want pity from you, the "pretty ones."
I just want a thank you now and then for being ugly. If not for me
would you be pretty? That thing you see running down my face are
not tears, it's spit given to me by one of the "pretty ones." It was given
to because I opened the door for her because that is what a man
should do. She turned back as she entered, spit on me, then laughed,
and all I did was say, "I'm sorry and you are welcome." So if you
ever feel depressed and sad that your makeup or your hair is not
perfect enough just be glad that you don't look like me and you can
laugh and spit on me all you want because it is not your fault that I
am ugly. The only thing I can say about me being ugly is, "That I
am really sorry for being me and you are welcome you are not."

VICTOR

'It doesn't matter if you believe that what I'm writing in this journal is true or not. I believe what I have seen but I can't tell the difference between reality and imagination anymore. The fragments of a past life haunt me.

Could they be evil souls trying to enter our world through the fractured reality of my mind? A reality they are further driving me into each day? Be careful, reader, because if your mind is weak, you could be next...'

~~~~~~~~~~~~~~~~~~~~~~~~

Tick Tock.

The old clock hanging on the wall points its arms at 2:53. It is too early to wake up. I toss and turn while the clock continues to play its monotonous two note melody. No mind trick like counting sheep has helped tonight. The clock noise rings in my ears as my senses strain against my will to catalog every sound, shadow, or smell.

Tick Tock.

My breath comes in gasps as the humid air feigns to fill my lungs with water, protesting with every inhale I can manage. This must be what it feels like to drown. How could so much moisture stay airborne? My ears are almost distracted by my gasping but the gears of that old clock mask my suffocation and drown out all other annoyances keeping me awake. Why do I still have that old clock?

Tick Tock.

I peel the sheets from my body and shift to a dryer spot. I glance at the clock and realize it has stopped ticking. I changed the batteries a week ago. I should not have bought the cheap brand.

An instant later the air rushes into my lungs and the sensation of trying to breathe underwater passes. I choke as my lungs soak up the oxygen they crave and then exhale in white puffs. Goose bumps rise on my shivering arms and my joints ache.

A deep voice whispers. "Victor."

Tick Tock.

The clock counts the minutes as the second hand continuously increases speed. They spin faster and faster while the deep voice calls to me a little louder. "Victor."

The room is spinning. Each time the voice calls, the spinning increases. It calls my name in rhythm with the ticking of the clock that is spinning until the arms become a blur. The voice becomes a constant buzz.

"Stop!" I scream but my voice is swallowed by the torrent of noise until I lose my breath. I find myself kneeling on the floor beside my bed as vertigo holds me down in the spinning room. My stomach lurches and my head swells with blood. The spinning slows and the voice no longer calls my name. My arms wobble as I lean forward. My stomach contents empty onto the floor. My head hits the cold wood and the spinning stops. My nostrils burn from the warm stench that wets my cheek.

My eyes open but I have to blink a few times to remove the sleep from the corners. I am in bed, wrapped in my soft dry sheets. The clock across the room was ticking silently and I was alone.

Glancing at the floor, there is no vomit. It felt so real. Maybe I am dreaming now and I was still lying in my stomach fluids and passed out on the floor. That had certainly felt real. I pull the covers to my neck and roll over. Maybe if I fall asleep in this dream I can wake from it. I need to clean my mess before it stains the floor.

Something touches my shoulder and after a moment I realize it felt like a hand. My skin freezes where the fingertips brushed.

I fight off the urge to leave the bed. The cold burrows further into my chest. My body becomes rigid as I notice the silhouette of a man standing at my feet. He is so tall that he bends to avoid hitting his head on the vaulted ceiling.

I open my mouth to scream but only a squeak escapes my throat. An unseen hand grabs my throat, squeezes tightly, and cuts off any further chance of a scream. I try to slip from the gripping force but it tightens on my vocal cords.

The giant tilts his head as he begins to sing with the same voice I had heard earlier. "Hush little baby. Don't say a word. Mama's gonna buy you a mocking bird."

I try to free myself as the silhouette leans across the bed towards me. The pain in my throat and lack of a good swallow of air is beginning to make me nauseated.

"Hush my child and let me give you that which is yours."

My gaze is locked on the creature as he moves around the side of the bed with an outstretched hand. The long arm is dark and has a grayish color across it. It stops inches from me. I try to blink tears into my drying eyes. The gnarled dry fingers paralyze me as they drift inches from me.

A blue fire pours from the shadows of the figure and runs down his arm. A scream catches in my throat as the flames engulf the hand. The palm is then pressed against my face. The flames cover my head and a frozen burst within the fire confounds me as it splashes against my skin.

The figure leans its head closer. "Do close your eyes and enjoy my appetizers."

My eyelids close, despite my struggle to resist the command. I feel the pressure in my mind as something bashes at the barrier to my inner thoughts. My walls shatter after a short resistance. Other people's memories flood my mind, nearly drowning my own. I could hear, feel, and smell everything in the hundreds of images flashing across my inner eye as if they had been my own.

People fought and murdered for love, for justice, and for freedom. They cheated, swindled, and stole to obtain selfish needs. Despite the good intentions of many, their cruelty only created chaos.

There are so many memories, images, and scenes playing through my head that it all begins to blur together into an unrecognizable mess. Somewhere, I hear someone cackling. The laughing overpowers the blending memories, distant, but near enough to smell the decayed breath.

My mind becomes too muddled to focus on the memories so I turn my attention to the laughter. The cackling continues to magnify until my ears ache.

As my mind spirals in places I do not recognize but feel I should, the laughter stops. The ragged voice penetrates the sounds of murder and rape. "Do you think my kind caused all of this?"

Uncertain of what the dark figure is referring to, I do not answer.

"No, you humans are truly the evil ones. You are like wild dogs ravaging a carcass and taking my offerings without any thought to what it might cost. It is you who have done more to usher in your own destruction than any of my kind could have ever imagined. You were made in his image and with that his limitless imagination. Our kind could never imagine such delightful cruel things such as you have. We weren't made for that purpose."

I feel smothered as my lungs sucked in the air with laboring gasps. The smell of decay was burning my nostrils. What is this thing talking about? Heat is building in my neck and head as a panic attack prepares to launch.

"Get away from me you piece of shit!" I spit the words at the monster.

The demon releases me and my eyelids fly open to the shadowy figure returning to the foot of the bed. There is no sign of the blue flames and no burns.

A fog creeps up from the floor and soon clouds the room. The mist thickens across the bed as it fills the room. Goosebumps rise on my arms as tiny ice crystals float across my skin.

The waving hand from the tall creature sends the icy mist into swirls that blow behind me. I turn and realize I am no longer on the bed or in my house.

A cold wet feeling in my shorts draws my attention to the dirty puddle I am sitting in. I pull myself up using a protruding brick from one of the walls lining both sides of the empty alley. Pipes with water dripping along them extend into the darkness above the lamps that line one wall for a short distance in both directions. The width of the alley is big enough to drive a large truck in but past the glow of the lamps is an inky blackness. A rusty old dumpster leans against the wall near the end of the lit portion of the alley.

Another scene bursts to life on the unlit wall. There is no projector or other light shining onto the bricks but images flow across the rough wall like a movie. I watch a moment longer as I recognize my own memory. I do not want to remember this.

Every attempt to break away my attention from the horrible images fails. My house burns while I watch helplessly in the street. A single act of carelessness robbed me of everything. I just want to end it all. No more pain, no more screw-ups. My lips feel salty but I swallow my regret when I hear faint sobbing.

So lost in my own thoughts so I barely realize the weeping is outside the memory. I follow the sound behind the dumpster.

A small girl huddles on the ground and shakes as she

cries. The aroma seeping from the cracked dumpster lid reminds me of an old vacation. I had been on the road for a week and forgot a package of thawing chicken on the counter.

I lean forward to get the girl's attention. Her head jerks up and we stare at each other for a minute. Her eyelids quiver as tears create a trail of mud from the grime caked on her face.

"Help me. Please I am lost and I want to go home." She whispers.

"Who are you?" I do not whisper because we are the only two people in the alley.

"I am Hope." She cocks her head to the side and stares into the darkened alley then lowers her voice to a point barely audible. "You must let go of the pain. You must let go of the man that took your family from you. You must forgive he who burned your house down with your wife and kids inside."

My clenching jaw aches. I have buried this in my heart for years. The thought of the criminal that I had carelessly allowed to take my family and my home from me sparked a fire inside me that threatened to combust through my pores. He deserves no mercy from me. Who is this girl to tell me to forgive that evil man?

"He got one year in a minimal security prison with parole in six months and only because he was related to a Senator! They said it was an accident!" I feel the dribble of spit that escapes my tightened lips but I do not care.

Hope stands and clasps my fingers. She tries to lead me, pulling me to walk into the darkened alley. I hold my ground and resist the light tug. There is no reason to ever let go, to forget.

The dark laughter echoes across the alley and a chill runs along my spine. I am not afraid but my head warms and my fists clench. I want to punch whatever is doing this to me.

In the corner of my eye, the dark figure emerges from

the shadows and says. "Come to me Hope and be lost to this human again." The inhuman depth of the voice softens my rage. My stomach knots as I concentrate on controlling my breathing.

Hope stares into my eyes and whispers. "Please find me."

I hang my head and my hand goes limp as she backs away. She tries to wrap her tiny fingers around mine but the pull of the shadow's call must be too strong. My heart sinks into my knotted stomach as she loses her grip and backs up to the towering shadow.

Again, I am alone as she is pulled from me. Her feet stumble as long burned fingers grasp a handful of her filthy blonde hair.

Maniacal laughter fills the alley as the dark figure turns and walks towards the darkness. She does not struggle but stares over her shoulder. I watch them go until they vanish into the shadows.

Am I losing my mind? None of this can be real, though it feels so real. I drop to my knees with my hands covering my eyes to stop the tears trying to surface. How will I ever overcome this pain? I let the tears flow between my fingers until I hear my own sobs echoing back to me.

The alley is gone. I rise to my feet and wipe the tears on my sleeve as I study the corridor I stand in. Doors line both walls and are evenly spaced twelve feet apart. Each door has a plaque with scribbles on it. The hall continues in both directions with no ends in sight and lined with doors in pairs on either side.

I examine the closest to me but the letters were smeared as if they had melted together. Across the hall, the plaque read "sorrow." The door creaks open on its own.

Inside is a long dark room with a single black candle burning with a reddish flame on the floor. At the threshold are five dumpy people hunched and staring at me. Their mouths are deep frowns and their long single eyebrow arches in the middle of their foreheads above egg sized black eyes. They appear as if they are on the verge of bursting into tears, then I remember the word on the plaque, sorrow.

The pitiful creatures scurry closer together without turning their heads from me. No sounds other than a little whine here and there come from them.

I cross the room, heading towards the candle when the light behind me dims. Everything falls into darkness as the exit is closed. The red flame is barely bright enough to glint off the large eyes of the miserable looking creatures that lurk behind me.

I wrap my arms across my chest as shivers run across my skin from the suddenly cold dark air. Then with a sudden burst of steam from the darkness, my nostrils are assailed by the putrid stench of rotting carcasses.

A soft glow carried on the spreading steam illuminates the room. Why am I here? I hold my nose to block the stench. I have lost everything. My family is gone as is my house and I have no friends. I resist the urge to lie on the floor and cry. Why am I suddenly feeling like this?

The pathetic creatures behind me begin to wail and cry. Their exaggerated moans wash over me. Steam comes from their mouths and now I understand what is happening.

"Your tricks can't keep me here. You can't make me into one of you. This is just a dream."

The sound of deep dark laughter turns my attention to the direction of the candle. Behind the candle is a throne with a back that rises into the darkness. The entire thing is made from human skulls wedged together. Sitting on the throne is the shadowy figure that has been haunting my dreams tonight.

Crimson shadows dance across the skull throne but vanish into the blackness of its occupant. I feel its gaze upon me. Deep rumbling laughter fills the room while the wailing creatures carry on. A pain burrows into my brain. My breath catches as I drop to my knees. I press on my temples, hoping to crush the pain out. Each cackle from the shadowy figure incites more bolts of pain. My insides convulse with every breath.

The laughter stops and the wailing dies. I take in a deep breath of the noxious air but not without my stomach revolting.

"What do you want?" The voice of the figure echoes all around me and nausea swirls in my bowels.

I stare into the shadowy orb that must be its head and reply. "Hope and some answers."

"Fool! You lost Hope long ago! Instead, I will allow you to ask me three questions and then you will leave."

The voice echoes from every corner and I wonder if the dark figure or something unseen in the shadows is speaking to me. "Who are you?"

"I am not Who. I am hatred. I am fear. I am anger. I am revenge. More than anything else, I am your desire."

"Why are you here?"

"You can answer that better than I, can you not? Alas, I will try to give you an answer since it is your question, after all. I am here because of all the suffering, pain, and hatred that humans have created. All the sins created by man have spawned my existence."

The sudden quiet draws me to glance where the wailers had been but they are gone. There is no visible exit. How many doors might be obscured by the darkness?

The rumbling voice from everywhere continues. "Do you remember when you were at work and accepted the phone call? They said your family had been murdered. You were unable to protect them. Did you not beg for revenge then? Through your hatred did you not call upon me? Did you not ask for his death when you heard the verdict of the monster who took your family away from you?"

The figure leans forward and I look to the floor. "Didn't you?" He whispers.

"Yes." I mumble.

Laughter rumbles as the figure relaxes into the throne.

I flex the muscles in my fingers as something inside me burns. The sweat on my neck cools the heat a little and my focus turns to the throne. I do not have to let this thing talk me down. I have already suffered for my loss. I do not have to suffer at the hands of this lying demon.

My voice is steady as I ask my last question. "Is there any hope for us?"

The laughter stops. "No!" The floor shakes and I squat to avoid toppling over.

I am thrown onto the floor by an unseen force followed by maniacal cackling. My ears ring from the volume of the obscene noise. Something presses me into the floor with increasing strength as the laughter continues. My chest is so compressed I struggle for breath. My arms are pinned. My mouth opens to scream but nothing comes. A warm wetness spreads from the crotch in my pants as my heart pounds, sending waves of pain along the blood vessels throughout my body. I choke as my lungs refuse to expand. There is no room to fill them.

A strangled scream slips from my throat and the force releases me. Panting for air as I open my eyes to find myself in my bed.

I peel the soaked sheets from my clammy skin and ignore the shiver running up and down my spine. Climbing out of bed but I find no vomit on the floor and the clock is ticking at a normal pace.

There are no little girls named Hope, no sorrowed figures, and no shadowy monsters laughing at me.

~~~~~~~~~~~~~~~~~~~~~~

'I wrote this in my journal in the hopes that you are stronger than I. This is only the beginning but you will not find me. If you ever find Hope, please hold on to her tightly and never let go.'

I'll Settle

I'll never be famous for my good looks, I don't have any.

I'll never be famous for my fashion, it's for the rich, and I am poor.

I'll never be known for my vocabulary, because I mumble.

I'll never be famous for having lots of money, I owe too many people.

I'll never be famous for any heroism, I will always try.

I'll never be famous for my many friends, because he died last year.

I'll just settle for being famous for all the things I'm not.

HOPE OF REDEMPTION

I wrap the shadows around my body as the subway train roars across the tracks under the city. I do not want the other passengers to notice my presence. The poorly insulated machine does little to block the cold winter night. I sense the slumbering humans above the ground, oblivious to the darkness that stalks the subway station we are barreling towards.

I have been traveling this world alone for a long time. My father's thoughts and intentions drift to me from a great distance. To him they are a whisper but my ears ring from the sound of his power. It is good that the humans are unable to hear the whispers he speaks to the world. Their fragile bodies could not withstand the power of his voice unfiltered.

I feel a dark presence lurking at the train station ahead, an evil that corrupts the very shadows. Dust flies as the breaks squeal like a thousand forks scraped across a chalkboard. And still, my father's voice pounds my ears over the noise.

Half of the lights in the station work and the other half flicker. The clock above the entrance is at 2:52:29. The breaks hiss as the train comes to a complete stop. It takes one second for the doors to open but the anticipation strains my patience. This moment is long overdue. I've waited for a century so this evil would come to me and now my champion is prepared.

The metal doors clank open after the gears protest with a grinding sound. My gaze is drawn to a corner of the station where a light that was not flickering a second ago is blinking rapidly. Then it holds steady and I see the beast I have been waiting on. Previously hidden in the shadows, his skinny six and a half foot frame fills the thin beam of light.

The filthy white t-shirt stretched across his muscular chest is ripped and full of holes so large that half the shirt seems to be missing. His blue jeans are loose and shredded and covered in mud and grime.

His skin is leathery and filthy where it is visible and his jaw is stained crimson. The riders on the train pay no attention to the otherwise abandoned station as the beast with dead eyes stares into the windows from the corner. His bloody lips open in an unnaturally wide smile to reveal a mouth filled with rows of pointed teeth.

His eyes bulge and he sniffs the air like a hungry wolf on the scent of a defenseless lamb. He remains still as his glare bounces from passenger to passenger. The left eye twitches as his gaze drifts across me but he will not be able to sense me. If he suspects my presence he will flee.

I take note of the passengers to determine if there is anyone that might cause the creature some hesitation. Three prostitutes are sitting together and eyeing a young college student snoring against a window nearby. I feel their intentions to convince the youngest of the three to distract him so the other two can pick his pockets.

The three women are watched closely by a large man with a gold toothed smile and sunglasses. He is their pimp and he plans to protect them if they are caught. He also plans to take most of the stolen money and sell the boys identity to his cousin.

Another woman ignores the rest of the passengers and constantly fidgets nervously with her barista uniform and the fake fur coat she has wrapped herself in. She does not usually travel the subway and the other passengers make her uncomfortable. She hopes the mechanic will finish fixing her transmission before she has to travel back to work in a couple days.

The last passenger appears to be completely asleep. He is near the doors and sprawled across an entire bench. Crumpled newspapers and bags of fast food are tossed all over him. He has been lying on that same bench for three days. I reach with my spirit and I feel his heartbeat strong and full of energy. He appears asleep or dead but he is listening and waiting.

I return my attention to the creature watching the passengers. His glare stops on the sleeping boy leaning against a window as the younger prostitute approaches him. Thick drool spills between the sharp spears and down his chin. He never blinks.

The creature lifts a bare foot and in less than a second he stands in the doorway of the train. His speed is far beyond what a human could see but not too fast for me.

A low laugh escapes from his maw, too deep for the thin frame. The laughter grows louder and morphs into a roar. All except the two sleeping passengers turn to the roaring maniac as the doors slide shut behind him.

The creature smiles as a thin purple tongue slides out of his mouth, licks along the sharp pointed teeth and then flicks the air as if tasting it. He grabs his hair from either side of his head and begins to pull at it. The skin on his head stretches and then rips from his left ear to the right corner of his mouth.

As the top half of his face peels off, he waves it at the passengers. The bloody yellow skull and eyes drip thick blood over his mouth. Blood rises at the edges of attached skin and streams down to his stained shirt. The skin remaining on his lower head is shaped like a horrid half smile.

Urine puddles on the floor under the pimp's seat and the air stinks with the smell of fear. Nobody moves but they drain of color. Their eyes are locked in the gaze of the creature and as he tilts his head, they mimic him. The only two not affected are the sleeping student and the vagrant, feigning sleep.

A gurgling voice slips from the razor sharp maw. "Let's play a game called…" He pauses and stares into the eyes of each passenger hypnotized by him. "Where is your soul?"

His purple tongue slides across his skull smearing the blood. "I need more of these." His eyeballs sag and then twitch back into their sockets.

The creature claps his hands together and then circles his sternum with his fingertips.

"Alakazam!" The ghoulish creature shouts.

Fingers plunge into his chest, ripping the worn shirt until his ribs crack. They dig deeper shifting the broken ribs. His fingers fan out inside his chest causing more ribs to fracture and snap. Blood oozes around his embedded hands and pools up from his throat and into his mouth. His tongue splashes in the pool of blood in his jaw and licks the stream that escapes his maw.

All three prostitutes faint as if on cue. The pimp and the barista stare with open mouths. Their breathing is shallow and I can feel their hearts slamming in their chests.

The beast gargles. "Aagaaga!" Blood splashes on the floor. "Here it is."

He leaves a mangled hole in his chest as he pulls out his cupped hands. The way his leer dances from face to face, he seems to think the prize is as precious as a boy would feel holding a lightning bug. He slowly steps closer to the pimp and barista and holds his cupped hands to them.

"Do you see the little soul I'm holding? Isn't it the prettiest little thing you have ever seen?" He waits for a response but gets none. "I need more pretty souls to play with so I hope you enjoyed these last few minutes of life because I have brought hell to you."

A giggle escapes his lips and his tongue flicks as if trying to pick who to start with.

"I want your soul to scream for all your sins. That is my pleasure."

The creature passes the homeless covered in trash and a grumble rises from the refuse. The vagrant stirs after days of laying still. His voice is deep and southern. "Who are you?"

The creature stops and turns to the poor slob. He roars and holds his arms palms out to his right and left. The breaks on the train screech and the train lurches in an attempt to stop.

The barista slips from her seat without attempting to break her fall and bangs her head on a pole on the way to the steel floor. The pimp grabs a pole to remain seated but does not remove his blank stare from the faceless demon.

A sulfuric smell fills the air as everything shakes. The windows rattle in their frames and the walls groan as if the train is splitting apart. The pimp loses control and vomit spews from his mouth. He falls from his seat and lies unconscious, sliding under the seats in front of him.

The train shakes as the demonic roar grows louder. The vagrant rolls his eyes and sits up. His long trash filled wiry hair droops down to obscure his identity.

"Who are you, you piece of crap?" He whispers with no hint of a drunken slur in his speech.

The demon stops roaring and stands to his full height. The train stops shaking and continues on its way. "Me? I am me. I am what fear is made of. I am why humans are afraid of the night. I am what rips minds apart. I am Na' and I am what you will fear."

Na' glares at the slob and then he realizes something is amiss. "How did I hear your whisper over all my noise?"

The vagrant stretches his arms, knocking most of the trash covering him to the floor. He leans back on the bench and rubs his bearded chin. He examines the bags of fast food but there is nothing edible. He pulls himself up using a pole to balance himself. He rises to nearly seven feet with broad shoulders. The demon is dwarfed by the size of the man.

The demon looks him up and down. I feel his thoughts recognizing the scar between his eyes but Na' is unable to remember where he had seen it.

The vagrant has grown in size and power since I last watched him merely fifty years ago. His time has definitely come. Father will be pleased, the champion will survive and pursue his calling.

Na's skin glows red. The sound of sizzling meat is accompanied by smoke rising from his clothes. Na's fists are balled and his jaw clenches. The wiry muscles bulge through the holes in his shirt.

The scarred man watches as clumps of dirt falls from Na's clothes. The lice in his oily matted hair pop from the heat.

"Who is not wise enough to fear me?"

"I no longer have a name, nor do I have any use for fear." The vagrant replied.

"What do you mean you have no use for it? Do you not feel my power? I am a demon and I will feast upon your soul!"

The homeless man smiles at him and reveals a mouth with many missing teeth. "You have come to feast on my soul?"

Na' steps closer and pulls back a fist. A growl escapes his boiling throat. His fist ignites into flame and lashes at the man who catches the flaming fist. The vagrant ignores the flames as they turn from reddish orange to blue.

"I will have your soul!"

Shaking his head, the man replies, "You have it backwards."

"My power is great. Only an angel can stand in my way and you are no angel!"

He smiles at the demon. "If I was an angel, I'd have lost my wings a long time ago. They call me Ranger and your power is nothing to me. I devour the souls of darkness. You've destroyed many souls, including the one you wear now which I was supposed to send to be judged. You have stolen too many from me and for that, you'll be destroyed."

"I have never heard of… how… you can't destroy me! I'm a soul eater. Why would you…"

Before Na' can finish what he is saying, the Ranger jerks his balled fist to the ground and twists until the bones in the arm break. The Ranger blasts his other fist through the hole in Na's chest and cracks his spine.

Na' gasps for air. "But we are brothers, why?"

"No, I'm not your brother. I'm not an angel cast from Heaven like you. I'm not on anyone's side. I've been cursed to walk this world in hope of redemption for the murders of innocents I caused in a past life. You've interfered with that job. That is why I stopped you from hurting these people. You might be powerful but I'm far beyond anything you've fought since your war in Heaven."

The Ranger sucks in a deep breath and then blows. Black dust floats off his clothes and swirls around Na'. The air becomes thick with the black dust for a few seconds before thinning and vanishing all together. Where Na' once lay bleeding there is the body of a thin youth.

Standing and lowering his head. "I'm sorry, I have failed you."

I lift the shadows that hid me and cross the train car with a warm smile. My appearance is of a young child so I am level with him on his knees. I place a tiny hand on his dirty shoulder to let him know I am here.

"No forgiveness is necessary, for you have served us well all these decades. We know that you regret the sins you committed."

I sigh, as Father impresses into my mind some new knowledge. "The Dark One knows that we are going to stop him from getting the fourth key to the Door of Souls. It hides the souls he has stolen from us, like this one." I point at the body at our feet. "He could have been saved if you had got to him first."

"With your permission, I would like to partake in the task of finding it." The Ranger lowers his head.

I hear Father's answer but I will not share it with the Ranger. "I will ask Father. I believe he plans to soon pardon you and send you home. You will be welcomed. For now, I must send you to retrieve something for someone. You should know that tonight you have aided us greatly by protecting that college student. His journey is just beginning and yours will soon come to its end."

I place my petite hands on both sides of his massive head and pull him to me. I kiss him lightly on the forehead. Tears stream from his eyes.

"Walk in our father's light."

"Thank you and the same to you brother."

The ranger rises and rubs the dimpled round scar and then looks at the people on the train. He says a prayer and then walks to the carcass. He tosses it across his shoulder as if it weighs nothing and stands by the doors. The train screeches to a halt at a well-lit station. As soon as the doors open, the Ranger is gone.

The passengers slowly wake up and glance at each other. I wrap myself in shadow and glide to the back of the train to observe.

"Did we hit something? Why am I under the seats?" The pimp asks. He pulls himself from under the benches and notices the vomit on his shirt and the urine on his clothes. "What the hell?" He rubs the bump on his head and winces.

The prostitutes help each other up and return to their seats. The barista pulls her coat around her and rubs a bump on her forehead. Her fingers come away with a little blood and her eyebrows rise.

"I need to go home…" The barista stammers. "to tell

my parents I love and miss them."

The pimp replies. "I think, no, I know I need to change." He glances at the barista. "My life." He begins to cry as he walks off the train.

The three prostitutes hug each other and cry. Their makeup smears and the youngest says. "I don't have anyone to go home to. Will you help me?"

The oldest of the three squeezes her hand. "If you help me get to mine."

"We have been through so much together the last few years that I feel like we are family." The last woman says.

The three women hurry from the train with the barista close behind. The doors remain open for a few seconds before the student stirs. He looks at his watch and barely exits the train as the doors close.

I lift the shadows from me and glide to the doors. "You have opened your eyes to your sins and realized that you must repent and go and walk in Father's light, especially you, young Adam Monroe."

I must move on to my next task. Father beckons me. I drift through the ceiling as the train pulls away from the subway station. I rise up from the ground in a park near the station entrance and then on into the cloudy night sky. The journey is a great distance but it is not a long trip for my kind.

The Past For Tomorrow

On the edge of my mind sits a sad little thought. My past sings a sad little tune in my ear that quiets all the thunder in my mind. I do not cry for all the things I remember because the past is what makes you better than you were. I cry because I do remember my past and tears should come at the end of a story not in the beginning. It is then when I should cry for all the things I should have done, not the things I did. I am not at the end of the story and that is where I want to be but I guess for now I'll just be a paragraph that has nothing to do with this story.

THE RIVER AND MY MADNESS: PART 2

Water gurgled over rocks and an eagle screeched high overhead. I sat and watched fish jumping after the mosquitoes hovering above the river. I jumped to my feet and grabbed for my guns as the trees rustled in the breeze. One of my revolvers was missing so I pointed the other at the woods where the burning doorway had been hovering.

It was not there. The scraps of burned wood and melted chains were also gone. I scratched my head and wondered if it had been a dream. My campfire was smoldering ash.

My vision swam and I stumbled a few steps towards the ashes while my head cleared. "What in hell? Was that a nightmare? Lord, please help me."

I kneeled and prayed. I had no idea what to say since I never really prayed except when Ma made us do it at dinner. I did not remember the prayer we said then since she died from a plague when I was seven. I asked for forgiveness and for guidance. I hoped amen was enough to finish it.

I moved to the edge of the river, leaned close to the water, and splashed my oily face. The cool water eased my tension and lifted the fog in my brain.

As I leaned over the river, my stomach lurched without any warning. Bile poured from my mouth and splashed droplets on my cheeks. Meat I had eaten the night before and something red with milky swirls drifted in the stream.

The redness faded to pink as it blended on its way downriver. I tried to rise when the pain in my gut shot to my groin and I bent over the water. More of the reddish liquid spilled and my nostrils burned. After a few seconds the heaving stopped and I took in a deep ragged breath.

My eyes watered from the burning vomit trapped in my nose. I plunged my head into the water and rinsed my nose and mouth. I rested on the smooth rocks and spit up water. My nose was aching but the stench was gone.

After setting my revolver beside the water, I crawled onto a shallow spot where the rocks were stacked like a bed and laid on my back. The water was deep enough to leave my face and chest dry. I listened to the trickling of the water as it flowed around me.

My booted feet remained on the shore. My hands were trembling. A shiver ran down my spine as an image of that thing underground flashed in my mind. The sun was already high in the cloudless sky. I closed my eyes to block the painful light. My weary muscles ached to lie still and relax.

A cool breeze rustled the leaves of the nearby trees as I soaked in the sun's warmth. After a while, the sunlight dimmed and I felt a few drops land on my head. Rain was coming, that would be nice. I needed to pack my things and find shelter soon.

When I opened my eyes the eyeless blond woman hovered a few inches over me. Through the strands of hanging hair I saw the sun was gone and the sky was filled with stars. I recognized her as the woman from the cavern, Victoria. The drops I had thought was rain were tears dripping from empty eye sockets.

She floated across the water and stood on the shore by my boots. I sat up and stared into the sky for a moment.

The sky was as black as black gold with the pinpricks of stars piercing the velvet. The full moon shined but its light was dimming. My old campsite was masked in a dark shadow.

Victoria spoke in a hollow voice. "Pray that you go to Heaven."

"I don't want to die."

"It's not up to you. All you have is a choice to either be on your knees or on your feet."

"But…" was all I could say as she faded.

Water clung to me as I climbed out of the river. I reached for my revolver but it was gone. I went to my hands and knees and sifted through the dirt and weeds but it was nowhere to be found. There had been no snorting or shuffling from my horse for a while either. I ran to where he had been tied but he was not there, just an old stump of a fallen tree.

A pile of cold ash was all that was left of the camp. Everything was gone. My horse, the rifle, both of my revolvers, my saddle bags and tent, and the rabbit trap I made was gone. Someone had robbed me. I needed to find someplace to sleep.

I marched into the woods, trying to stay as quiet as I could with my boots clacking against the rocky terrain. Coyotes would not be easy to deal with now that I have no guns or fire.

The ground shook and I stumbled as branch-like appendages burst from the ground a few feet away. It looked like five thick tree trunks in a semi-circle but as it grew I realized it was in the shape of a giant hand with its palm facing up. Trees and huge rocks were shoved to the side as the chair shaped wooden structure rose up. The palm of the thing was large enough for a full grown longhorn to stand on.

The smell of sulfur drifted from the hole left underneath as the roots spread to dig into the ground. I pinched my nose and stepped back. Fires burned from the pit that the chair had settled above.

An inky shadow drifted across the ground. It flowed around my boots and slid towards the chair. It carried the stench of rotting meat. After drifting up the side of the chair, it rose to take on a humanoid shape. It was the same thing I had seen in the cavern, sitting on a throne of skulls.

The fires made its rotting skin seem to glow red. The smell of sulfur and decay was so strong I could taste it. I was struck in the chest and knocked to the ground. I could not see what held me down. I felt the pressure of five finger tips digging into my ribs.

Leaves and dirt piled against my right side as the invisible hand turned me to face the throne. I tried to look away but another invisible hand grabbed my chin and turned it towards the figure on the wooden throne. The fingers tightened as I resisted and I felt as if my jawbone would crack. I shifted to try and stand but something grabbed my feet and arms. It held me tight.

That same cackling I heard last night echoed from the woods. That was the same laugh that I had heard from the cavern. I stared at the towering figure as it sat and watched me struggle. The hands lifted me and then shoved me down on the ground. My hair was pulled back till I was looking up at the wooden throne.

As the laughing ended, the figure spoke with a deep voice. "That is how you should always greet me, boy."

"This ain't really bowing, not that I'd bow to a demon, ever." I grunted.

"You will always bow to me. Someday I'll devour your soul and then you will know that your resistance was for nothing. Then you will finally understand my power over you."

I gritted my teeth together and replied. "Let me go."

I closed my eyes and prayed. I never really knew if I believed in Heaven or Hell but now I have no doubts that there is some kind of Hell so there must be some kind of Heaven. I silently asked God to save me.

"Boy!" The demon roared. "Do you not realize I already own your soul. All that praying is a waste of time. Don't fret. I'm not ready to consume you yet. There are some things I need to take care of first so I must leave you soon. In the meantime, I have a gift for you."

Something thudded next to me. I was concentrating on not losing my bladder and trying to ignore everything I had heard. "I don't want anything from you. You're a lying piece of shit."

There was no answer and the hands released me. My mouth was full of dirt so I remained still for a while. There was no sound and then I heard the chirping of a bird in a nearby tree. I opened my eyes and squinted at the bright sunlight pouring through the branches. I was lying by the smoldering campfire.

There was no devil's chair nor a scary demon anywhere. My horse stood by the old stump I had tied it to. My revolvers were both in their holsters and my rifle was by my side. I shaded my eyes from the bright sun. I could tell it was midmorning.

I jumped to my feet and fired my revolvers in the direction the floating door and the devil's chair had been. A cricket landed too close to me and I fired a round at it. Then I fired at leaves dancing across the ground.

The revolvers finally clicked on empty chambers, I dropped them and fell to my knees. I do not know what had really happened to me or if it happened at all. Relief washed over me as I thanked God for saving me.

After I gathered my wits together, I packed my gear and saddled my horse. I needed to get as far from this river as I could. I climbed onto my horse and just as I was ready to spur him on, I was blinded by reflected golden sunlight near the river.

I hopped off the horse and walked to the shiny rock that was lying in the dirt. It was filthy but there was no mistaking it for anything other than what it was, a golden nugget. It was as wide as a silver dollar.

I washed it in the river using both hands to make sure I did not drop it among the stones. Then I saw the glinting gold shining in the water. I pocketed what I had and carefully plucked the five nuggets scattered among the stones.

I went to my horse and placed them in the bottom of the saddlebags. I rushed to the river and found a thick stick to dig and dislodge the stones. How much gold had been sitting right here under my nose?

I considered spending the rest of the day digging in the riverbed. In a few minutes I found a couple more. I found eight nuggets from the size of a bullet to a silver dollar.

What if I could find a bigger piece? I would be set for life. I could play poker with the rich men and satisfy the young women at the inns with the red lamps on the porches. Food would no longer be a daily struggle. No more trapping rabbits for stew.

As I was sloshing in the water, I had the feeling I was being watched. I glanced and saw a man standing on the edge of the river watching me. His bare chest was reddish brown. His pants and moccasins were beige and a single feather was tied into his waist-length black hair. There was a huge scar on one of his shoulders that looked like an oversized wolf had tried to rip the limb off.

He had made no sound when he approached or I had made too much noise playing in the river that I had not heard him. I wondered how long he had been there. I glanced at the water and then at my saddlebags on the horse. Why was he here?

I looked back but now he was sitting ten feet from the riverbank with his legs crossed. His chocolate colored eyes seemed to be analyzing my every move. In his lap was a tomahawk and a bow was lying beside him, within easy reach.

Lines in his face ran down both sides of his mouth and he did not smile or frown at me but his brows creased closer together as I stared at him. I realized I was holding the heavy stick like a club so I stormed onto the shore with it held high. I would never reach him before he could throw that tomahawk. Tossing the useless thing away and pointing a revolver at his chest seemed like a better idea.

"You can't have my gold and I'll kill you if you try and touch it. Now leave before I shoot you."

He made no move to rise. His eyebrows rose and he crossed his arms. My finger twitched and pulled the trigger. The gun clicked but did not fire. I had not reloaded after shooting at the shadows earlier. That must have been what had drawn him to me. I unclenched my jaw and lowered the gun.

He spoke but I did not understand what he said. It could have been Cheyenne but was different than what I remembered. Finally he placed his palm on his chest. "Little Tree."

I pointed at myself and replied. "Jacob Monroe."

Then Little Tree spoke in Cheyenne which I had learned enough of in my youth to understand. "I journeyed two snowfalls. The spirits sent me to warn you. You throw rocks back in Wolf River and leave this place."

He did not smile like it was some kind of joke. He uncrossed his arms and laid a hand on his tomahawk.

Heat burned in my chest because I was certain he had come to steal my gold. I used what little Cheyenne I could remember. "You leave. I reload gun and then put more holes in you than rotten log!"

He replied in English. "I'll leave. I have done what I was told to do. Remember, Jacob Monroe, if you not leave Wolf River before sun falls..." He then frowned and continued. "Evil spirits haunt this place and if you wake them, you will never rest."

The pouch on my holster that kept the bullets was in my hands in an instant. I flipped my wrist and popped open the chamber. I tried to place a bullet in every chamber but dropped a few through my trembling fingers.

Dropping them only fueled my frustration. I was going

to enjoy every hole I put in that lying native. He had come to steal my gold. He wanted me to throw them back so he could pluck them out for himself after I had gone.

The gold was mine, it belonged to me, and I found it. I will be dammed if I let some thief steal it from me. I flipped the chamber closed and pointed the gun where the native had been. He was gone. He had left as quiet as he had come.

I fired three shots into the woods. "They belong to me. The gold is mine!"

I wiped the sweat from my brow with my sleeve and holstered my revolver. Then I swaggered to my stick by the river. As I stepped into the water and prodded the ground until a nugget the size of my fist rolled next to my boot. I dropped the stick and grabbed it.

As I lifted it from the water, the refection of the sky turned dark and a freezing wind blew across the river. My skin tightened as the intense cold spread across my wet clothes.

Thunder rumbled in the sky and then I was covered in water after a blinding flash. I could not tell if it was raining or the water had been displaced before I was swept into the river until the water was waist high.

Cold wind pressed on my backside and I could not stop shivering. A cold presence leaned on my back. Then I heard a hollow whisper. "I told you to…"

I spun and drew my revolvers to shoot this new thief. The gold is mine and nobody is taking it from me. I fired with each gun. "It's mine! You, the Indian, and anybody else can all go to hell!"

Victoria hovered above the water and turned from me. "It's not the gold I wanted. I wanted to save you but now it's too late." She cried.

The dark clouds parted and the stars and moon were shining brightly. That cannot be possible. It was morning.

Victoria vanished and I knew then she was right. I dropped my revolvers in the water. I had already lost the big nugget but I did not care anymore. I had condemned myself to the short road to hell. I waded to the shore and fell to my knees.

I had been given a choice but I failed. I had given in to my greed and was willing to murder for wealth. I dug my hands in the dirt. Tears fell to mix with the mud.

I rose and grabbed the saddlebag with the nuggets in them. There were no nuggets in my hands. They had all been large round black stones. They burned my hands. The heat bit into my skin as smoke rose from the stones.

Black stones scattered on the ground and a screamed escaped my lips. My hands were red and already swelling.

"Boy!" That deep voice rumbled. "I am here for that soul you've been flavoring for me."

"It's not my fault. You tricked me. You knew I wanted that gold. You did this to me. You made me want the gold. It's your entire fault."

"My fault? No boy, it was you who lusted for the gold. You saw what you wanted. You wanted to kill for it and then you wanted more. I gave you the chance to leave. Victoria warned you and she wasn't the only one. You couldn't control your actions, I did nothing."

Darkness crept in. The stars and moon dimmed till they were completely gone.

"Come on you piece of shit. I'll fight you with everything I have."

The voice answered with a whisper. "What's the matter? Can you not see me? I am standing right in front of you."

A blue light flashed and outlined the silhouette of the demon. It stood directly in front of me. It towered above me as my head reached its abdomen. Shadows shifted as I tried to focus. Its eyes burst into blue flames.

A massive fist moved towards me. "Here, this belongs to you." The demon insisted. "It is the thing you have lusted most for a long time."

The shadows slipped from the hand to reveal decayed

and burned flesh barely covering the bones. Smoke was rising between the fingers. I felt my hands go numb as the fingers opened to reveal a glowing stone a little smaller than my fist. At first it was blue then it changed to gold.

My hand twitched. This gold nugget was the answer to my dreams. No more digging and traveling. I could buy a tavern where I could drink whiskey and play poker all day. It was pure and perfect gold.

"If you really want it, all you have to do is take it."

Dreams of whores and money clouded my mind. I was no longer afraid or angry. I needed this nugget. I must have this nugget. I slowly took the gold and grinned at the large twisted metal chunk.

"I will be back." The demon sneered.

I heard the words but I was not really paying attention to it anymore. The demon turned and left. I saw then that the blue light was coming from the portal. It was open and the inky blackness inside swirled with shimmers of blue light escaping the darkness.

The demon bent and stepped into the gateway which slammed shut behind him. There were no chains on the door. I glared for moment, forgetting the gold in my hands and watched as flames burst from the wood and crumpling it like paper. It blackened and the ashes blew into the wind.

I stared at the empty air for a second before the weight in my hand reminded me of what was really important. I felt a hunger in my heart. I no longer wanted the whore, the whiskey, and the gambling. I needed it.

A soft cold breeze blew across my neck and reminded me of Victoria.

I heard a soft muttering. "Jacob."

Why was I so obsessed with this gold nugget? I searched the campsite for the blond ghost but there was nobody else there.

I saw my own breath puff into a cloud as the breeze returned and with it another whisper. "Why did you take it? Where was your faith?"

I stared at the gold nugget gleaming in my palm. I threw the nugget into the river, along with it all my dreams and desires. I hoped the feeble attempt would earn some forgiveness for my failures.

As soon as the nugget hit the surface of the river the water erupted like a stick of dynamite had gone off below. Water and stones battered me and I threw my arms up to protect my head.

My clothes were soaked and dripping. The water churned and boiled where I had thrown the nugget. That blasted door rose from the river. My heart pounded and I searched for my horse. Running felt like a really good idea.

The door flew towards me and stopped within a couple feet. Sulfur and rotting wood gagged me as I inhaled.

Behind me that deep voice boomed. "Did you lose something?"

I dropped to my knees and prayed to a god that I know must exist. My Pa used to tell me, "There could be no darkness if there had never been no light."

"Boy! Don't ever believe that you have a chance of being saved. Your soul is a tasty meal that I am hungry for. Stand up and take what is yours."

I rose and turned to the shadowed figure standing over me with rotten claws outstretched. The gold nugget reflected the sunlight right into my eyes.

I shook my head as I stared at the beautiful gold. "I don't want anything from you ever again."

"You don't have any choice in what is going to happen. Your fate is sealed. Now, take this!" The demon smirked. It opened it palm to reveal two blue eyeballs with their bloodied roots dangling between his fingers. I felt my stomach heave. I knew those were Victoria's eyes and I struggled to keep whatever was in my stomach down. I bent and clutched my abdomen.

The demon kneeled with me. "Don't waste that, here, let me have a taste."

I lost control and the acidic burn of bile rushed up my throat, into the demon's hand and onto the gold nugget. I heaved as the demon licked its fingers with a long forked tongue, making sure to clean the gold. I had nothing left to empty but I could not stop heaving.

The demon patted me on the shoulder. "Don't worry; I'll give you something to eat."

It tossed the gold nugget over a shoulder and then poked one of the soft organs with a boney finger. White fluid squirted and it flattened.

"Nope! Not in here."

Then it licked the remains of the eye and swallowed it. It slurped on its fingers, showing me its grotesque rotten face. Its eyes burned with a blue flame as they seemed to bore into my soul. I tore my gaze away as fast as I could.

The demon moaned. "Mmmm, delicious." Then it punctured the other eyeball with a fingertip. "Ah! There it is."

It pinched the eye and fluid squirted on my pants and its wrist. Along with the fluids was a little golden ball. It was the size of a marble.

The demon rose. "It's almost done." The humorous smirk that had donned his expression was now a stern glare. "Open up."

I tried to retreat but the door had moved to block me and the heat from it singed my hair. The demon grabbed my throat and held up the ball.

"Let us begin."

It slowly put the gold marble to my lips and pressed against them. I tried to fight but it felt as if my teeth were being ripped from my gums. The marble slid between my parting teeth. I tasted iron when it rubbed across my tongue. I gagged and resisted but that rewarded me with a more intense taste of the bloody thing.

The demon almost seemed to purr. "Doesn't it taste so grand? I know it does."

Then the marble was at my throat and the finger

pushed it on. I tried to cough and spit but the marble was shoved through my resistance. The taste of burned and spoiled meat hit my tongue and I realized that his rotten finger was in my mouth. I gagged on the rancid flavor. My mouth dried and then felt like it was full of ash as the marble was shoved into my throat.

"Swallow it." The demon leaned closer to me until my vision was filled with the two flaming eyes.

I kicked and clawed at the demon, trying to push spit to the back of my mouth to flush out the marble. As soon as I did, it slid past my tongue and I had to swallow or choke on it.

"That wasn't so bad was it?" The demon pulled his finger from my mouth and laughed.

My stomach cramped but I was not sure it was because of that marble or the disgust at having that rotten finger against my tongue. "Lord. Please let me wake from this nightmare and forgive me for all my sins. Please Lord, forgive me!" I begged.

The demon continued laughing. "I forgive you, my slave."

I shook my head and put my hands together as he released my throat.

"What do you think you are doing? Are you trying to pray to some other god? I told you it was too late for that. You are mine to toy with as I please."

I opened my eyes and tried to spit but only a glob of blood came out and landed at its feet. I glimpsed and noticed the feet were cloven hooves before the shadows that shrouded his body drifted down to cover them.

"Oh, let me have some of that." The demon said as it wiped the blood with a finger and plucked it into its lipless mouth. What flesh was left in its cheeks then turned into a grin. "That was tasty. I hope you have more to whet my appetite with."

Bloody drool seeped from my mouth as I stared at the demon. I was numb to its taunts. I wanted to flee but I knew it would not matter anymore. The demon had won.

"Maybe next time."

"No." I mumbled.

The flames in its eye sockets burned a little brighter as it leaned towards me and wrapped its long bony fingers around my throat. "How can you say no to me? I own you and I can play with you for as long as I let you live."

As it released my neck, I slumped to my knees. The demon stomped to his exit. I heard the door slam and felt the heat as it burned into ash. Then the ash burst, tossing me into the mud.

I stayed there and fell asleep under the shining moon with my face in the mud and tears flowing to make sure the mud never dried.

I woke with the sun burning on my neck and my stomach full of lead. When I shifted it felt like my bowels were full of butter knives. I climbed onto my hands and knees and shoved a finger to the back of my throat until I emptied my stomach.

I wobbled a little but I was able to get to my feet. I stared at the blood, stomach acid, and a little red marble lying in the mud at my feet. I swayed and realized the cramp in my stomach was still there. I do not remember when I had last eaten. How many days had I been sitting by this damned river?

Something landed behind me and then I felt claws rake across my back. I twisted away thinking it was a bear. The demon was over me without the shroud of shadows masking his body. His chest had no skin; it was an empty ribcage with a swarm of flies swirling inside. Thousands of tiny eyes were focusing on me. The legs had two sets of knees. The lower set was inverted above blood covered cloven hooves. There was no place on its body that was not rotting. The skull was hairless and the skin hung on like worn leather in the bright sun.

The corners of his mouth shifted into a sneer as his hairless eyebrows bunched into the center and hung over his eyes like a sun visor. The flames were gone and his streams of smoke floated into the air from the empty holes.

"Did I tell you to throw away my gift?" The demon hissed.

I tried to be strong but my heart was pounding and I struggled to control my breathing. "How did... why... what is... how are you able to be here in the daytime?"

The sneer vanished and the demon laughed loud, clamping its hands over its chest as the flies bounced inside him, buzzing with anger.

"Did you think I existed only at night? Sin never rests, boy, so neither do I. I'm just patient. However, I'm offended that you would reject my wonderful gift."

I had nothing to say. My back burned and I knew there was no point in moving. This demon was going to do as it pleased. I said a silent prayer that it would end this torment soon. I was too tired to fight.

The sneer returned as the demon growled. "Don't worry, Jacob Monroe, I don't need you anymore. You are going to be a father and so I have a fresh and innocent baby to play with. I promise he will have all the good things in life but you won't be around to see him. You are going to die soon."

I remember the woman in town that I laid with last and I knew it must have been her. Unlike most of the women I had been with, she was not a whore. We had spent a month together and I had left without a word. She had said she was in love and I could not stay and disappoint her by pretending.

"I'm going to be a father?" I was at a loss for any other words.

"You do remember that woman with the nice round ass and big tits? Well that's her. She got pregnant and she'll name the boy David. He's going to be a chip off the old block, I promise."

The demon lifted the red marble and held it to my face.

My vision blurred as the burning in my back increased to a spasm and then fell to a dull ache. The marble became cloudy and then something moved inside.

It was the woman I had been with, lying on a table and surrounded by other women. Her legs were propped up and she was screaming as the other women focused between her legs. A tiny baby boy covered in blood and afterbirth was lifted into the air. The woman reached for the boy as the women cut the cord. The marble clouded as the woman held the baby and cried.

The demon smiled as it closed its hand around the marble "Did you recognize her? You broke her heart. It's a shame that you left her after she poured her heart out to you because she still loves you. She thanks you for giving her a boy."

I choked on my words and trembled as I finally realized what the demon was planning to do. I could only hope to live long enough to warn her and save my son.

The demon walked to the hovering doorway over the water. "Do you want me to tell your son anything?" He called, with his back to me.

"No! He will defeat you!"

I will never know if the demon heard me or cared. I rolled onto my stomach and crawled to my saddlebags to find this journal. I do not have much longer to live because the cuts are burning and I feel the chills and a fever sweat setting in.

If you find this journal, bring it to Victoria Monroe. Please help a father who failed to protect his son.

To Laugh

To laugh in the morning is easy but to laugh at night is the hardest thing I have done. I can smile at the morning sky and tell a joke to the sun as it rises; I can even sing a happy tune when I walk outside. A happy thought in the morning is a thing that grows into a smile. The morning sun is a happy thing that fills the room with a glowing anticipation of possibilities. Night time is the thing I hate the most, because it's the time to remember all the things that went wrong in my life and it will play over and over again in my dreams. My mind will race with the things that are trying to slow me down and at the finish line a wall will be waiting for me. When I finish racing, the clock is the thing that I hate because it slices away my life and my sanity. During the night is where my life is wasted and that is where my life reminds me how much I am not needed. At the end is when I laugh again.

THE MARBLE AND MY FAITH

Telephone poles zip by my window as I count them. My favorite challenge is to memorize the number of plates from each state but there are no license plates this far into the countryside. I have to do something to stay occupied on my annual and uneventful journey to visit Grandma. There is nothing but flat treeless fields as far as the eye can see across this part of the Texas panhandle.

I have not seen Grandma in months. There is plenty of studying to do with finals only a few days away but I needed to get out of the city for a while and think about the direction my life is headed. The farm my Grandma has lived on her entire life is the most peaceful place on Earth. When I work with the animals, I can be alone with my thoughts.

It is the perfect place to sort my ideas and explain to Grandma that I want to make my life more meaningful. My grades are top of my class but I lost all interest in running a business. It is not enough to make money anymore. I want to make a difference in someone's life. Not just one person but as many as I can reach.

Grandma is the only person that matters to me and I hope she thinks it is a good choice to go to seminary school. I fear she will say the whole idea is a huge mistake.

I never was very religious but in the last few weeks I have felt a pull towards something I do not fully understand. I sat with a friend and argued with him that there was no point in anything. He gave me a bible and showed me some verses to read in the book of Proverbs.

The bible talk really made me uncomfortable. I was not sure why it bothered me so much because Grandma always quoted verses to me when I was young. There was always a verse for every situation.

After a few days of avoiding him and the bible he gave me, I gave in and read. I realized the man who had written Proverbs had also been wondering what the point of life was. What was the point of building and growing if everything eventually dies and is forgotten?

Sleep became difficult and I was no longer focused in class. Grandma made me say my prayers at bedtime and meals when I was little but after I left for college, it felt silly to keep it up. I never really believed any of it mattered anyway.

A couple days before the summer break, I finished the book of Proverbs and decided to pray for answers. My mind fell at ease for the first time in weeks and I got a full night's sleep.

When I woke, my decision was made. I would go into the priesthood. My insides churn with guilt as I consider that I might have had this calling for years and ignored it.

A flash of lightning in the distant twilight startles me from my memories and for a moment a blue light hovers where the lightning had struck the ground. It seems to be moving across the flat fields along with the bus. It must be an afterimage from the lightning.

The little hairs on my neck stand and my skin ripples with goose pimples. Then I feel the presence of someone leaning over my seat. I jerk my head up but the only person nearby is a snoring old man two rows back.

My imagination is toying with me and the strange blue

light is gone. My gut tells me something is still watching me. Rubbing my eyes, I block out my paranoia.

Every dollar I earned when I was young, every penny from every lousy job I had to get between classes, was spent on college. All of that was to get the degree of my dreams. I was determined that someday I was going to run a business but I no longer felt the desire for it. Instead, I feel a higher calling and I need Grandma's acceptance to know if I am making the right choice. Guilt crept into my heart for already making up my mind without discussing it with her.

A soft glow expands over a low hill with young trees as the lights from the closest town to Grandma's farm reflect off the stormy clouds above. I push away the nagging sensation of someone staring at me and force myself to get a power nap in before I arrive at the bus station in a half hour. I miss Grandma and the last thing I want is to sleep on the drive home.

Squealing air brakes wake me from my dreamless slumber. The handfuls of people on the bus are making no motion to gather their belongings. Most folks avoid returning to this sleepy old town once they have escaped. I grab my bag and sling it over my shoulder as I rise and step into the walkway.

A young man in fatigues emerges from the darkened rear of the bus and nearly shoulders his way past me. I trail behind the soldier and think up excuses for his rudeness. He is probably exhausted after traveling so far from whatever base he came from. The soldier moves quickly and I pick up my pace and follow him off the bus.

It does not take long to find that gray haired bun on top of Grandma's head. I walk beside the bus to make my way to her. Her back is to me as she carries on a discussion with a middle aged couple. Grandma has always been friendly and almost everyone knew her in every town near the farm.

"Welcome home, Adam." a warm breath whispers across my ear. Startled, I turn my head towards the breathy voice to find nothing but the side of the bus with all the windows closed. I continue to turn in a complete circle and realize there is nobody else near me. A shiver runs through me involuntarily. Who was that and where did they go?

I hurry across the small parking lot to add some distance between the bus and me. Grandma has her back to me. The couple is engrossed in Grandma's conversation as I approach.

Once I am within ten feet, she turns and smiles. How does she always know when I am sneaking up on her? Throughout my childhood I was never able to surprise or hide from her.

I break into a run, dropping my bag, and dive into her open arms. Forgetting her strength, she squeezes the air from of my lungs with her farm-hardened arms. She is warm and her hair smells of freshly baked cookies. After a couple of minutes of holding each other, she grabs my face with both hands and kisses my cheeks and forehead. Before I can protest, I find myself suddenly wrapped in her arms again. As she finally releases me, I take in a deep breath of the fresh country air. The breeze smells of honeysuckle and grass.

"I thought you weren't going to let me breathe for a second there," I jest.

There is no waver in Grandma's smile as she replies. "Don't tell me all that school work in the big city is making you soft."

With a quiet laugh, I shake my head and grab my bag. I scan the parking spaces for her old beat up red Ford but it is not there. So instead, I follow Grandma as she strides into the parking lot. The years of farming have made her tough and despite her many years, she walks as briskly as a young woman.

As we approach a huge, shiny, brand new silver Chevy

pickup, my heart leaps. The parking lights flash as she points a black key fob at it.

I barely realize that I stopped in my tracks with my mouth hanging open.

"Grandma! When did you give up the old truck?"

"I sold some stocks. I'm just getting too old to drive an old truck that keeps breaking down."

"Sold stocks? When did you start investing?"

"As soon as that insurance policy came to me after Grandpa passed away."

"That was before I was born."

"Get in the car boy."

I can feel the engine purr more than hear it. My Grandma has a brand new truck. This thing must have cost a fortune. Had she been rich all my life? I thought she had spent her entire savings on my education. That was another reason I was worried she would be unhappy about me dropping out.

She steers the giant pickup onto the farm-to-market road. "If you have had all this money for so long, how come you never hired farmhands or sold the farm and moved into a little house somewhere?"

"Idle hands are the devil's play things, dear."

A barking laugh escapes my lips before I catch it. She always says that. I thought it was to keep me working on my daily chores. I never thought we had a choice in the matter. I guess it was a good distraction after losing Grandpa. Grandpa was not a subject that came up a lot while I was growing up.

She is as tough as a well-worn saddle but she could be as soft as a breeze on a hot summer night when she needed to be. I had to learn the hard way on how tough she could be.

No matter what, Grandma has always been there for me. While growing up in her house, I learned quickly to stay out of trouble. Living on the farm taught me many life lessons and I always considered myself a good thoughtful person because of it.

The truck turns smoothly onto the dirt driveway that leads to the Victorian style two-story old house on the top of a hill. As the truck comes to a complete stop, I unbuckle myself and step into the gentle breeze. I Inhale as much of the clean country air as I can handle without making myself dizzy.

I grab my bag and head to the wooden porch that wraps around the entire house. The steps creak under my feet and at the top I lean against the rail to enjoy the air for a moment longer. The smell of freshly cut grass and the sweet honey scent from the Mexican plum trees float on the breeze. The odors are so different and more pleasant than the acrid city air that I have to fight off the intoxicating scents and remind myself that there is a purpose for my trip.

I rush into the house and up the stairs to my old room. The first thing I do is empty my dirty clothes onto the floor and then unpack my only clean clothes, two non-matching socks. Grandma always likes to do my laundry. She made sure I knew how to take care of myself before sending me off to college but she enjoys spoiling me so I let her.

While sorting the lights and darks into two piles, Grandma steps into the doorway. "Baby don't worry about that right now. Come and sit outside with me and have a big glass of iced tea. We can rest and you can catch me up on your schooling."

A sigh escapes as I listen to her steps descend the stairs at the end of the hall. "I guess it's good to get this over with early," I mutter.

Grandma smiles at me as we rock in our chairs and inhale the country air which I have missed so much. The breeze has cooled in the last few minutes since we arrived.

It is best I just get to the point. "Grandma, I'm going to change schools. I want to become a priest."

"I think that would be great, boy."

Her gaze remains locked on mine and I sense the sadness in her eyes that I have begun to notice the last couple of times I have visited. I almost feel as if she somehow knew what I had been going through these past few months. Out of fear of making her worry, I had not mentioned to her the troubles in my heart.

She rises gracefully from her rocker, grabs the pitcher of tea, and kisses me on the forehead.

"Baby, I'm going to get supper ready so finish up your tea and relax."

"Love you Grandma. Will there be any dessert?"

Just as the screen door swings shut behind her she replies. "Cookies."

After a few minutes of staring across the fields and the farm-to-market road that winds its way between the low hills, I lean my head back and gaze at all the tiny stars that never grace the night sky of the big city. The sound of Grandma shuffling pots in the kitchen reminds me of where I am. For a minute, I feel like I am ready to drift into the stars.

"It don't get much better than this." I speak to the twinkling lights of suns far away. It feels real good that Grandma did not try talking me out of it. She seemed upset but she would have said if she opposed my decision. She always shares her opinion when she disagrees. That is why everyone loves her so much. You always know where she stands.

After a while, the smell of baked potatoes and buttered corn drifting to me is too much to resist. I go into the dining room as Grandma is setting the plates and silverware. Grandma looks at me with the shimmer of fresh tears reflecting light from the hanging lamp above the table.

"What is it Grandma?"

"Just memories of when your dad brought home your mom. She wore a pretty blue dress that matched her eyes. He was so nervous about bringing her to meet the family."

She tells me the old story of that night my mom charmed Grandpa but my mind wanders on to memories of all the times Grandma told me this story. Her voice feels like a warm blanket soothing my tired and stressed mind.

After listening to several other stories, I stack dirty dishes to help clean. Grandma waves me away from my dirty plate and scoops it up before I can argue. She is as quick and nimble as I remember her to be.

Halfway out of my chair, she sets down a full plate of homemade oatmeal walnut and raisin cookies. Each cookie is bigger than my palm and thick as a slice of bread. I grab one and stuff half into my mouth without a word.

While I cram in a couple more cookies, Grandma tells me that a fox had been killing some of the chickens a couple weeks ago. She had to get a roof put on the coop. A couple months before the fox came, two of the cows broke the fence along the highway behind the land. One of them decided to stop traffic by wandering into the road. Luckily nobody was injured, everyone honked at the old girl not realizing she was deaf.

Jim Towers and his four sons took twenty minutes to lead the old cow from the road. They mended the fence as good as new and the cows have not escaped since.

As I wipe off crumbs from the fourth cookie I could not help but laugh at the thought of any of the old cows directing traffic.

Looking at her watch, Grandma gasps and bounces to her feet.

"It's already eleven thirty. I can't believe it's that late. Baby, I have a lot to do in the morning. You need to get to bed as well because you have a few chores, too."

"Okay, Grandma, I will. Love you."

She scoops up the plate as I grab more cookies to stuff into my already swollen belly. She kisses me on the forehead and smiles.

"I will see you in the morning."

On a farm you learn to go to bed with the sunset because you have to wake up with the sunrise. It is not a good idea to wake up late. The animals would get impatient to start their daily routines and the work on the land would get harder as the day gets hotter by the hour.

I watch her clear the table of the leftovers while humming to herself. After a few minutes of her scrubbing dishes in the sink, I accept that she will not let me help clean. I wander into the living room where the shades of the large bay windows are pulled open to reveal several acres of grazing fields.

Sliding the window open, I inhale the fresh breeze as the moonlight dances across the grass while fast moving clouds play hide and seek with the full moon. How dare these dark ominous clouds hide such a beautiful site on my first evening back on the farm?

Sitting on the couch facing the window, I stare at the moonbeams and enjoy the fresh air as I slowly drift off to sleep. I forgot how quiet and peaceful the country can be.

I awake at what sounds like a cannon going off in my ear and for a moment I am unsure where I am. I must have fallen asleep on the couch. Grandma must have closed the window when she checked on me before she went to bed. She worries I would get sick from sleeping in the night air. I need to remember to thank her in the morning.

After a few seconds, I am falling asleep when I hear the sound again. A marble bounces and rolls unnaturally loud across the wooden floor. The sound is magnified by the total silence.

Then it stops. I settle in to return to dreamland when it continues again. I try to ignore it and pull a couch pillow over my head.

After the fifth time it hits the floor, I realize there is no way I am going to sleep until I make it stop. It must be a mouse playing with some old marbles inside the couch.

This is the country, after all, and there are plenty of mice. The thought of a mouse crawling under the same cushions I am resting on drives me to my feet.

The moonlight is bright enough for me to find the switch on the wall. As I flip on the light, the noise ceases. I get on the floor in front of the couch to listen closer but I hear no sound. There is no scratch or rustle of a mouse attempting to hide.

With a quiet groan, I pull the couch from the wall quick enough to hopefully catch a glimpse of the offending rodent that must be slipping into a hole. To my surprise, there is nothing but a rectangle of dust the same size as the old couch. The Towers boys must be sweeping for Grandma.

Climbing onto the cold floor, I then slide an arm underneath the couch to feel for any clues. Rubbing along the underside of the couch, I find that there are no holes in the thin cloth that is stapled to the bottom. The entire point of the cloth was to prevent rodents from hiding in the springs.

I find no clues around the baseboards. There are no little footprints in the thick film of dust, not even a disturbance from a rolling marble.

After shoving the couch against the wall as quietly as I can, I scratch my fresh chin stubble with my dusty fingers as if the action might assist in solving the mystery. I decide to get some rest instead. Flipping off the lights, I head down the hall to my room when I hear it again.

Tap, tap, tap.

The marble bounces and rolls across the floor. I shrug my shoulders and rub my stiff neck and then close my bedroom door. It has to be my overactive imagination. All the stress of my uncertain future must be getting to me.

Jack Sparks is the name of that rooster with his cock-a-doodle-doo right outside my window this morning. I have been gone too long although the sound makes me feel at home. He is much better at waking me than the annoying beep of my alarm at the dorm. It would be less horrible if he would not do it on my window sill at the first break of dawn every morning.

The day that baby chick arrived on the farm I fell in love with him. I named him Jack Sparks, after a character in my favorite book growing up. He is feisty and he always seems to know when I am home.

Grandma told me that when I was at college he never climbed onto my window sill. I guess that means he loves me too.

He was almost renamed supper six months after we got him. Grandma was trying to fix some wire on the chicken coop when he decided to protect his hens. The crazy rooster went straight for her legs.

That only happened once. I had to get between them to stop her from removing his head with the axe and pluck him that night. Somehow I was able to convince her he did not mean it and that he mistook her for a coyote.

Jack realized his mistake too. Ever since then he has made sure to keep as much distance from Grandma as possible. He rushes out of the chicken coop when Grandma goes in to collect eggs and stays on the opposite side of the pen when she throws seed.

While I am thinking of opening the window to shoo him off, I smell bacon and Grandma shouting from downstairs. "Breakfast is ready!"

Glancing at the digital clock on my little night table, I realize she let me sleep in. It is already 6:07 AM. The bacon aroma invades my nasal passages and I toss the covers aside. I take a quick sniff of my armpits and smell something that could be mistaken for cooked ground beef. There is time for a quick shower.

Stepping into the hall I acknowledge her. "Be a minute Grandma!"

I grab a towel from the hall closet and then slip into the bathroom. Tossing the towel on a rack above the toilet tank, I notice the white paint has begun to peel in various places. I need to add that to my list of chores in case Grandma has not.

I check my nose hairs and the shadow of my beard coming in as the smell of the bacon wafts across into the bathroom. My stomach responds immediately with an audible and painful gurgling growl.

The shower is quick. I was becoming spoiled with hot showers in the dorm while here on the farm there is nothing but ice cold well water. There is nothing in the world that will wake you faster than jumping into a shower that runs on underground water. After a short rinse, I quickly dry myself. I notice that the medicine cabinet is ajar.

"I don't remember opening that."

Shrugging my shoulders, I dry the last wet spot on my ankles before hanging the towel on the towel rack. Then I slide on a pair of jeans that Grandma must have washed last night and hung behind the bathroom door.

I open the cabinet for my toothbrush but my hand stops above the toothpaste. A little dark red colored marble is sitting next to it. My mind races back to the incident last night. I stare at the solid red sphere for a few seconds as my mind struggles to process some connection between that red marble and last night. Snapping out of whatever self-hypnosis I was losing myself in, I find the marble in my palm and drop it in a pocket. It is odd that I do not remember actually picking it up but I cannot keep that bacon waiting any longer. Where did I leave my shoes?

Taking in the scene of the quiet little kitchen before entering all the way in, my breakfast is steaming on the stove. I smile at the overflowing plate of bacon, eggs, sausage, and toast. It looks like Grandma is making sure I will have enough energy to complete the chores she has left for me.

Bowing my head, I say a prayer of thanks for my meal. I apologize for forgetting to do so last night. Then, as I lean forward to dig in, I hear a soft male voice whisper my name from behind me.

"Adam."

The hairs on the back of my neck stand but before I can turn to where the voice came from, the front door squeaks open and slams. My gaze is locked on the hall as Grandma enters the kitchen with a big smile and the local paper rolled in her hand.

"Just went to check on the pigs. Did you sleep well, sleepy head?"

Making herself comfortable in a chair across the table, she waits for my response. After glancing over my shoulder and seeing nothing, I dismiss the voice as my imagination. First that moment I got off the bus last night and now this? No more ghost movies for me.

"Yeah, pretty well. I had to go to my room last night. Some mouse kept playing with a marble and was keeping me awake. I tried looking for it but I didn't see a mouse anywhere. I couldn't figure out where it was coming from."

I get a glimpse of her trembling hands before she drops them in her lap. She is a shade paler than usual and her smile is fading.

"Baby, it must have been a dream. Now, when you're done, put your dishes away. Here's a small list of stuff I need you to do if you would, please."

Her eyes almost seem to haze over as she pushes the list towards me. I watch her leave the kitchen and then listen as the door swings shut behind her.

What happened? Grandma went from cheery to tense in an instant. I had never seen her fuss over a little mouse.

The list that she made is pretty light work today. Maybe she is going easy on me because it is my first full day back after several months but I have not grown soft in college. I dismiss her strange reaction to the mouse story and plan my day around the list.

There is always plenty of work to do so I do not understand why the list is this small. I will be done by lunch. Maybe she planned something special for later today.

A couple of years ago I tried to convince Grandma to hire help for some of the tougher things since I was heading off to college. She had said that she was no longer a "Spring Chicken" and I could not help but worry.

Our closest neighbor, Jim Towers, is a family friend and he has four big boys that all farm with him. Grandma told me that when she called, Jim would drive the quarter mile down the road and bring a son or two to help her. I hardly had to encourage him to look out for her when I left.

A cloud of dust rises from the old Ford pickup approaching in the driveway. I toss seed to the chickens and I still need to get the eggs. It is not like Grandma to let me sleep in and though my list is short, I am late in getting the animals taken care of.

The truck stops behind Grandma's truck and an old grizzled man with a short well-kept gray beard hops out of the driver side. I grin at the sight of Jim Towers and two of his sons. I could not tell who was who. The two blonde headed young boys with matching faces tumble from the passenger side, pushing and shoving at each other with laughs.

The smaller of the two lands on his rear which encourages more laughter as old Jim slaps his own knee with a straw hat before plopping the flimsy thing on his graying head. He tips the hat towards me then makes his way to the porch where Grandma is already standing and smiling at him warmly.

Grandma lightly hugs Jim and then they stroll towards the rocking chairs. Jim was born and raised on his land and he and Grandma always got along well.

Bob, who is a year younger than I, and Sam, who was a

year younger than Bob, were wrestling on the ground. After a little while Sam is crying "uncle" while Bob straddles across his chest and punches him in the shoulders.

I haul the bag of chicken feed in a rusty wheel barrel to the shed on the side of the chicken coops. I make my way to the hen houses with a basket to collect eggs. Grandma and Jim sit and enjoy tea while the two boys unload paint brushes and a can of paint from the truck bed. So Grandma did plan to paint the bathroom after all.

Although Jim is seven years younger than Grandma, the farm life has taken its toll and he looks older than her. Ever since he lost his wife ten years ago, he has come to visit twice a week for tea and talk. I suspect all those visits are not because he is lonely.

I gave Grandma my blessing to go on a date with him. "I see the way you look at him when he visits and you always put on a nice dress."

She laughed and threw a rag at me. "I can dress any way I like and besides I am too old to be running around like a little school girl putting on makeup and batting my eyes at boys or waiting for a boy to call me."

Despite Jim's protests, Grandma always paid his boys an honest wage for the jobs they did. At first they had fought it because their Pa had told them to not let her pay them. When she tipped them an extra twenty or fifty dollar bill, depending on how tough the job was, they agreed to keep quiet. Grandma never took advantage of his kindness and made sure the boys got what they earned.

The boys often refused to let her pay when they came without their Pa. They would instead sit in the kitchen and talk to her about girls and other things boys would have discussed with their mom, while she made them a good hardy lunch and a cherry pie. Some days Grandma would send them home with an invitation to bring Jim for supper.

As I finished with the chickens, I sat in the coop

among the hens as they pecked at the seed and Jack Sparks chased a few that caught his eye. I watched Grandma and Jim sit and chat on the porch sipping at their tea while I pretended to watch the rooster.

She seemed so at ease as they stared at each other. When Jim looked away for a moment, her gaze drifted and her smile faded until he spoke and regained her attention.

It is unusual for her to be so distracted and I could not help but think it had to do with what I told her at breakfast. Why did it bother her so much? It was probably all my imagination. Maybe she had mouse problems lately and she did not want me to know.

After Jim and his sons had gone home and I found the leftover paint from the bathroom. I unscrew the rusty hinges of the screen front door and lay it down to begin the repairs. Sanding the rust till I find the steel underneath and then smoothing it with a layer of molding putty does not take me long but I will be sore tonight. Then after the metal filler dries, I sand it till it is flush with the rest of the hinge. The tedious task eases my mind as I concentrate.

I would have done this job earlier but Grandma needed her space and she had been sitting on the porch with Jim all afternoon. Bob and Sam had done a good job in the bathroom. I dip the brush they left into the can and then apply a thin coat over the hinges until they look brand new.

Grandma slips quietly past me without a glance in my direction. "I'm going to fix dinner." Her frail voice has me worrying.

Hovering around the chicken coops and avoiding the Towers boys, I had floated through the day in a daze. Now that they are gone, I am left with time to think. Why would a mouse and a marble bother her? There has to be more going on.

Next, I remove the screens and sand the paint for the entire frame. I quickly brush paint across the wood and then lay the door down to let the breeze speed up the drying.

Sitting on the steps while I wait, I gaze at the trees swaying in the distance. There might be a storm tonight but I was not as good as Grandma at foretelling the weather.

The smell of meatloaf drifts through the doorway and my stomach attempts to do a flip to remind me that I need sustenance.

After the paint dries, I screw the frame into the doorway and squirt the hinges with oil. I put everything back in the shed, including the paint and the freshly cleaned paintbrush.

There is no sign of Grandma when I enter the kitchen a few minutes later. A plate of meatloaf, corn on the cob, mashed taters, and green beans is on the table. A small piece of paper lies next to it. She left a note?

'Baby, I'm not feeling well. Going straight to bed.

I love you.'

The food is not as satisfying without her to keep me company so I shovel it in my mouth. Afterwards, I put away my dishes so I can check on her.

I sneak along the hall to her room and find her door slightly ajar. Tiptoeing close to see if she is already asleep, I hear weeping. Through her tears, she is saying a prayer. I put my ear to the opening.

"…please Lord, hear my prayers and let this pass."

My cheeks burn for spying so I sneak away. With nagging marble thoughts pushed aside, I walk into the living area and watch the darkening fields outside of the open bay windows.

The sun sets as dark clouds roll in and chase away the last of the sunlight. Small shows of lightning dance around the house. Each flash allows me to glimpse the fields as clear as when it is day. The rumbling in the distance is followed by a soft cool breeze blowing into the windows. There are many miles between the storm and the farm.

I must be really tired because I do not remember

sitting. The tension releases into the wind as my head falls back on the couch. Once again, the breeze and distant thunder rock me into a deep sleep.

KRA-KOOOM!

I jump to my feet like a terrified child as those yellow fangs of a giant dog chasing me on my bike still make my heart race. The images slip away as quickly as they had come. Was that old nightmare what just woke me?

No, it was thunder that almost made me soil my shorts. The windows were rattling and my heart was pounding fast and hard. The rattling stops and I take a few deep breaths to calm my nerves and collect my thoughts. I had fallen asleep on the couch again.

The windows vibrate a little from the thunderous booms. I have never seen the house tremble from a storm. Several threads of lightning flash from the ground up to the clouds and shadows dance along the walls. Ground to cloud lightning scares me a little. I would not have recognized it if I had not dated that girl who was studying to be a meteorologist. She was obsessed with lightning.

There is a lot of electricity in the air but the presence I sense watching me is why I feel little hairs rising all over my body. I search the room from where I stand but nobody is here with me. My imagination is really toying with me lately.

A tall dark figure appears in the fields. His burning eyes are visible from two acres away while the rest of his head is shrouded in darkness. The balls of blue flame trap my gaze like a fly in a spider web. My legs will not turn from the window despite my desire to.

Thunder booms with a bright flash of lighting arching in between us. My vision goes completely white. I stumble from the window as my legs return to me. Blinking repeatedly, my sight slowly returns. An image of the lightning bolt burns across my retinas. I rub my eyes for a minute but that does nothing to solve my sudden blindness.

I risk a look as my vision returns but the tall strange figure is nowhere to be seen. My mind feels as if it is full of mud. There is no way I saw a man with burning eyes. I am tired and the lightning is making me anxious.

"Just a bad dream."

I do not remember falling asleep but Jack Sparks is all too eager to wake me with the sunrise. Almost falling out of bed, I realize my shoes are on and my clothes cling to me with a day's worth of hard working sweat.

Why am I not wearing my sleeping shorts? The most comfortable clothes I have ever slept in are my undershorts inside out. Maybe this has to do with the nightmare last night. I need to stop falling asleep so early and make sure my shorts are on before bed. My funk drifts to my nostrils to remind me that I need a shower.

Wait, how did I get to my bed? The last thing I recall is falling asleep on the couch and then having a nightmare. It felt so real but it could not have possibly happened, could it? No, it was a nightmare like all the rest.

I will not share last night with Grandma, not after the way she reacted yesterday. With no sounds coming from the kitchen, I assume Grandma must have slept in. I will be quiet in the shower. If she really was feeling sick, she will need her rest.

As I finish getting cleaned and dressed, I open the door to be struck by the sweet smells of bacon, eggs, and biscuits. The growls from my stomach are becoming a common response to the aroma of breakfast every morning.

In the kitchen, Grandma sits at the table with her back to me. She lifts a shaky hand to take a sip of her coffee as she stops whispering. I am not sure what she was saying or if she was praying or talking to herself. I hope she is not becoming senile but that might explain her strange behavior.

My shoe squeaks on a tile and Grandma nearly drops her cup. As if I had not surprised her again, she recovers quickly and returns her attention to her coffee.

"Grandma, are you ok?"

"Of course I am, you just startled me, that's all."

"Sorry Grandma, I smelled the bacon and was hypnotized by it."

The corners of her mouth lifted a little but only for a second. "Well sit down and eat the eggs, bacon, taters, biscuits and grits I made."

"That's a whole lot of breakfast."

"You're a growing boy."

"I'm 23 years old."

"You'll always be my baby boy no matter how old you are. How did you sleep last night?"

Afraid of frightening her, I dismiss the urge to tell her about the nightmare. "I think I slept wrong because my neck is stiff."

"Good, good, thank you Lord, thank you."

"What do you mean? Good? This neck is going to bother me all day."

She glances at me and gives me a warm smile before she replies. "I mean it's good that it was not worse, that's all. Now hurry up and eat because I need you to cut the grass while I'm in town buying some hay and feed." She sets the mug on the table and continues. "When you're done and if I'm not back yet, there are some cold cuts and chips in the fridge."

She rises and kisses me on the forehead before leaving the room.

My fork hovers over the aromatic breakfast that is causing my stomach to rumble with anticipation. I am not sure what that nightmare was and why I can remember it so vividly. It is as clear in my mind as any memory. Grandma seems almost relieved when she thinks I am not having nightmares. Why would that bother her so much? It was not the first nightmare I ever had and they never bothered her before.

Placing my fork on the plate, I say a quick prayer of thanks for all the good things I do have and then another for Grandma. I should pray more often, not only when I feel helpless.

Once the prayer is done, the food vanishes in a matter of minutes as I expertly shovel every morsel into my throat. My stomach thanks me and my taste buds sing from the savory flavors. There really is nothing as good as Grandma's home cooking.

After finishing off the extra helpings sitting on the stove, I clear the dishes and pans and wash everything so Grandma will come home to a clean kitchen. It is the best thing I can do to thank her for cooking these wonderful meals for me.

Once the dishes are dry, I run down the hall to Grandma's room to get the key to the shed. She always leaves her keys to the house on the nightstand. A beam of morning sunlight peaks through the curtains of the otherwise darkened room. The light is enough to make my way without stubbing my toe.

As I step around the edge of the bed to where the beam of light was focused, I notice a streak of dirt that trails into the shadows under the bed.

"She must be upset for her to leave a mess like that."

On my knees I can see the trail leads to a small metal box wedged under the railing and at the edge of the darkness. Dragging it from under the bed, I am stunned. It is completely metal but covered in mud and rust that is spread across its surface. It is roughly the size of a hat box, nearly a foot tall, over a foot wide and a foot deep. I lift it to test the weight and it feels close to twenty pounds. There is definitely not a hat inside.

The case looks to have been dragged out of a muddy swamp or sewer. It was covered in patches of mold, weeds growing from the hinges, and dozens of small dents all around it. A musky wet smell drifted from the mess covering it.

Holding my nose and looking closer I can decipher six numbers stamped into the lid.

20-32-2-24-4-2

There is a sliding bar on the latch that looks rusted shut except for the fresh scrapes along its length that reveal it had been opened recently.

The bar slid much easier than I had expected from a lock that looked to be more than a hundred years old. Inside is a spool of pink thread, a few arrow heads, three exotic looking feathers tied to a wooden stick, a small black bag, a worn leather journal, and a giant canine tooth. The tooth was large enough that it must have belonged to a wolf of some kind. The small black bag was filled with a strange black dust that burned my nostrils as if it was giving off some kind of heat. What is all this stuff for?

Lifting the thick journal into the sunlight, the words "Read Not" are visible and burned into the cover. I stare into the box as my mind races with questions of why Grandma would have all this weird junk under her bed. Maybe this box is the cause of her recent mood change.

"What the Hell?" I say under my breath.

I pull the box into the pool of sunlight beside the bed to get a better look inside. The interior of the box itself is in far better shape than the outside. Since everything is dry, the box must be waterproof. It is a little dull and worn and there is a little dust covering everything but otherwise nice and clean.

As I set the journal aside, some newspaper clippings slide out of it. A couple of photos are mixed in with the old faded paper. I squint at the writing to find clues to this strange mystery.

Wherever this box came from, Grandma must have recently dug it up and pushed it under the bed. Why would Grandma not share this with me?

I skim over the clippings but there are too many to read.

"…a man walked into town and claimed a monster had attacked him near a river. A few hours later he died from a wound on his back. Local officials believe the slashing wounds might have been caused by a grizzly…"

The paper is brittle so I handle it gingerly to avoid ruining it but when I search for a date, the paper edge ends before the year. All I can see is it was written on November eighth. The pictures and the writings are antique.

If I linger too long, Grandma will catch me snooping. I better put everything back and get to work. I gently lift all the clippings on the floor and place them inside the cover of the journal. My curiosity is piqued and I decide to mention this mysterious box in the morning.

As I grab the last article, someone sits on the bed beside me. My head jerks up as my heart leaps in my chest. Grandma smiling at me from the corner of the bed was not quite what I was expecting. My body is frozen and I lock on her gaze realizing I have been caught.

"Baby, go ahead and put it back in the box and put it under the bed."

"What is all this stuff?"

"My mother took me to see my grandfather the day before he died and he gave me all of this. He was in a state mental hospital because they told us that he was insane. He told me this box was at his home waiting for me in the basement and that I needed to go get it. It is a record of the men in our family and I needed to give it to you when you were ready."

"What? How would he know about me before my dad was even born?"

"He didn't say your name knucklehead. He meant to my first male grandchild. I was nine years old when he told me this and he asked everyone to leave so that he could talk to me privately." She fishes with her hands and stares at a corner of the room as she continues. "They had him strapped in a jacket and chained to a wall. After everyone left he told me that everyone thought he was crazy but I could tell that he was a sane man. His eyes were steady and focused, not like the shifty or nervous eyes of everyone else I saw in that hospital."

The pain in her heart became visible as the lines around her mouth deepened with a scowl. I had heard talk around the town when I was a kid that he had gone insane hearing voices and that a demon was after him. Now that I'm older, I have come to believe that he suffered from a severe case of paranoid schizophrenia. The anguish in Grandma's expression hits me in the solar plexus like a boxer's punch.

Guilt creeps into me as I realize that all these years I assumed that he was crazy. The stories made it seem obvious but Grandma never believed it. Her cheeks are wet and I fight the urge to cry with her as she goes on with the story.

"He was just upset that his son, my father, had died when I was 2 years old. I remembered him by the photos that mother showed me. He told me the real reason why my father died wasn't heart failure as everyone had said. If I really wanted to know more I would find answers in the box."

"What was the real reason he died?"

Her tears run freely across her cheeks as she stares at me, holding my gaze as if to make sure I am really listening. Then she hesitates and shakes her head. "Baby, when I pass away you will have all the answers you'll need."

"That will be many, many years from now. I don't want to wait."

"Go cut the grass like I asked you to do, please."

For a moment I feel the heat of anger rising as I realize she is going to keep this a secret from me. I force down the useless emotion and stand. After grabbing the key off the nightstand, I hug her tightly before I go.

Stepping into the hallway, I hear her praying quietly. I

bow my head and say a quick prayer for Grandma so things can go back to the way they were before I ever mentioned that stupid marble or found that stupid box.

As the sun rises throughout the morning, my clothes stick to me and my exposed arms redden. Despite the beads of sweat pooling from my pores, my throat feels like it is stuffed with cotton. I ignore the discomfort as my mind stays focused on the weird things going on at home.

Why would my great-great-grandpa want me to have this box and all that junk in it? Why is Grandma making me wait till she is gone? It makes no sense. There must be a clue or maybe an explanation in that dirty old journal.

With that journal on my mind all morning, I drive the riding mower in squared sections until I reach the front yard. When the sun is at its peak, my stomach begins to growl and my parched throat is begging me to wet it.

Grandma sits in her rocking chair and stares at the fields where I dreamed of those fiery eyes. She does not seem to notice the roaring engine as I park by the porch. I climb off the mower as the engine shuts off and skip up the steps. It takes a minute before she realizes I am watching her and she smiles. This is the second moment in my life I have approached her without her noticing right away, the only times she did not see me long before I got close.

"Baby, you look hungry. There's a meatloaf sandwich and some lemonade in the kitchen."

"Thanks Grandma."

Entering the kitchen, I find nothing. The bacon and rolls were on the stove from breakfast but there was no sign of lunch. Helping myself to the cold leftovers, I get my fill. After lunch, I take a longer path to the mower around the back of the house. I do not want her to feel bad or lie to her about that meatloaf sandwich.

That box has to be the cause of all this. My need to discover what is in there is overwhelming, as it may be the key to help her get better.

Hours drag on before I finish the huge yard. The sun hovers beyond the hills and paints the sky pink, orange, and purple. Grandma is no longer sitting on the porch after I park the mower in the shed and run to the house.

I tip toe inside. The clock in the hall shows that it is a little after seven and time for dinner. I sniff the air but there is no delicious odor floating through the house. The kitchen is cleaned and empty and the leftovers are stored. There is no sign of Grandma.

"That box must really be disturbing her."

Opening the fridge, I find some of the ingredients I needed to make my famous dorm sandwich called the Big Daddy; sliced ham and turkey, a head of lettuce, a tomato, some strawberry jam, the jar of mayonnaise, and the jar of sliced pickles. Taking three slices of bread from the bread box by the fridge, I go to work on making my meal.

My stomach growls and threatens to eat itself as I cut and squeeze everything together. There are several other things I would usually add to the sandwich but there is only so much to work with in Grandma's kitchen. I sigh at the pathetic sandwich. I am going to call this one Little Daddy.

I grab a pitcher of iced tea and pour myself a glass after putting away the unused food. That was thoughtful of her to make some tea today. Maybe she is not as under the weather as I had suspected.

A bag of potato chips in the pantry would top off the meal so I toss it on the table and then dive into the sandwich. It has been a while since I have made a sandwich and it tastes wonderful. I devour the food, wipe crumbs from my shirt, and then clean my mess.

Once the kitchen is back the way I found it, I pour another glass of tea and plop in front of the TV in the living room. After surfing quickly through the seven fuzzy channels that the old antennae can pick up, I turn it off and toss the remote to the opposite side of the couch. The curtains are open in the bay windows and a shiver crawls up my spine with memories of the nightmares.

Setting the tea on the coffee table in front of the couch, I stand and stare at the fields. With a shrug, the childhood fears are dismissed as I open the windows to let in the breeze. I shiver in the chill air.

There is a low rumbling in the distance as the soft wind continues to brush across my skin. The flashing lights tease me with promises of a good rainy storm tonight.

Nothing can be heard from the animals in the barn, no matter how I strain my ears. There is nothing, not a coyote howling, no crickets or frogs making music, and not a single snort from the barn. My gut quivers at the odd silence, apart from wind and thunder.

Grass trimmings and a few leaves collected along the porch below the windows swirl in miniature cyclones. The scent of rain is in the air.

Drifting into sleep, the howling wind stops and I feel as if I have been submerged in icy water. My breath puffs in white clouds as goose pimples swell on my arms. The sudden silence magnifies the normal ringing in my left ear. The annoying sound is usually drowned out by every day noises.

Rising from the couch and staring through the bay windows, my blood races. Am I having that nightmare again? The same dark figure stands in the fields. Those glowing blue orbs pierce the darkness and shroud the rest of its features. The lightning skittering across the cloudy sky cannot penetrate the hovering blackness.

My breath catches as it rises above the ground and begins floating towards me. I must be having a night terror like the ones we studied in psychology. Trapping me in its fiery gaze, it rises higher until the bottom of the lightless silhouette is level with the window frame.

I scream at myself to close the windows but no sound comes and my body remains paralyzed. My hands tremble as the shadowy thing grows. My lungs seize up so I concentrate only on pulling air in and releasing it. My fears overcome whatever holds my eyelids open and my eyes shut just as the shadow reaches the railing of the porch.

Waiting feels like an eternity. I am uncertain as to what is coming. The only thing left, it seems, is to look to God. If I am going to go into the priesthood then praying when strange shadowy blue fiery eyes float to me would be the logical thing to do.

"God, I know this has to be some kind of nightmare and I'm praying to you that it is. It has to be. Give me your strength oh Lord, and protect me. Amen."

I listen to the deep rumbling in the distance as the lightning flashes are visible through my eyelids. My eyes open one at a time and my breath puffs in white clouds as if the house had been dropped in a deep freezer.

I am seated on the couch in the darkness as I realize the lightning has moved on and the moon is obscured by thick clouds. A quick rub along the fabric confirms it really is the couch. The blackness of the room makes my hair stand on end. It must have been a dream. I need to find what in my life is causing these night terrors. This one really got to me because the feeling someone is watching me remains.

Laughter fills the room, a deep metallic bass sound that no human could naturally make. The small amount of light from the windows fails to beat back the darkness as the shadows creep towards me. I stand to get my bearings and flip on a light.

I feel it before hearing it. Something strikes me from behind and knocks me onto my hands and knees as the floor rumbles for a second. Jumping to my feet and spinning to see what assaults me from behind, there is only darkness.

A cold wind blasts through the open window and nearly sends me back to the floor. Leaves and grass cuttings ride the powerful gusts around the living room. The roaring wind becomes intense and deafening as the debris forms a small tornado. My ears ache as the cyclone pulls at my clothes.

I begin to worry that Grandma might come to investigate the noise when debris smacks across my cheeks. I blink too late as dirt grinds into my cornea.

Wiping my eyes until the tears flush the dirt from them, I realize all of the noise has stopped. As my vision clears, I am stunned to find myself in the dark but there is no dirt or other outdoor debris and the wind has died.

This must be a dream. How do I know if I am awake or not? What is happening to me? Stumbling across the dark, my shin bumps against the couch at the same moment the front door blows open. Debris filled gusts burst into the hall and living room.

I squint enough that my lashes protect my vision. The dark silhouette of a man surrounded by shadows appears in the doorway beyond the swirling filthy air. The eyes are orbs of blue flames and the rest of the body is nothing more than shadows hovering behind.

I gasp for air. The smell of rotting meat fills my nostrils, almost forcing me to heave. I realize the face is not a shadow but is a burned skinless skull. The muscles and tendons along the jaw flex and stretch as I feel the gaze penetrating into my mind, my soul.

My gaze locks onto those flames. The bluish light spreads before them and surrounds me and the air warms enough to remove the chill from the tempest. The temperature continues to rise as the fireballs bore into my skull. Sweat beads from my pores as the heat intensifies to a suffocating level.

Willing my eyes to close, I pray silently for the strength to overcome my fear and whatever this thing is that has me in its grasp. The heat is suffocating while the icy fear growing inside me counters the inferno.

Laughter fills the room with the deep echo of wailing and screaming touching at the edges of amusement. I want to cover my ears but my arms do not respond. My chest aches from the pounding of my heart.

"Please God, forgive me for not having enough strength. Forgive me for not having enough faith." I whisper.

As the words are spoken I feel a relaxing sensation throughout my body. What is happening? The raging fire is still present but it no longer hurts. The strength of my arms and legs has returned. What was overwhelming heat has now transformed into a comfortable summer breeze.

As I pray thanks for my renewed strength, I feel stronger and my heart begins to pace itself. My breath calms. The priesthood is exactly where I am going. There are no doubts as God answers my prayer and the fear evaporates.

Raising my voice to shout. "Our father..."

The cackling stops abruptly, startling me to silence for a moment, as a deep rumbling metallic voice interrupts me. "Boy! Do you think that your prayers bother me in any way?"

I stare into the eyes of this creature that mocks my faith. Anger seethes from the depths of my soul. An inferno threatens to consume me.

With gritted teeth I answer him. "Yes! You should be afraid!"

The rumbling voice softens. "I'm here to help you, boy."

"Help me?"

"To help you achieve everything you've ever wanted. Women, power, money, anything."

"How are you going to do that, take my soul?"

Its mouth curves into a bloody grin as the laughter begins again, the sound of a choir of ghosts screaming in agony under an avalanche of rocks. The laugh cuts off as the demon roars. "Boy! That's already mine. I'm just not ready to collect it! You've yet to fill it with sin. You will give into the temptations so that I can savor its delicious flavor. You have no choice in the matter. The decision was made before you were born."

As it floats closer to me, a shadowy fist rises. I try to step back and though my strength grows, I am rooted in place. The smoky clawed hand opens with its palm up. Resting in the center is the same little solid red marble I found in the medicine cabinet.

"Here is your inheritance and the way to everything that you want. All you have to do is take it and claim what is rightfully yours. Within it is your every desire, your every wish."

I become obsessed with the swirling fire that swims inside and a sensation overcomes me as if I am falling into the orb. I push away all thoughts other than the swirling flames.

"What do you mean? How's a marble going to make my dreams come true?"

"It's the key to your every desire. All you need do is hold it, wish, and it will come to pass."

"I don't want it and I'll never take it, for God is the only thing I need!"

The figure floats from me; his cracked and bloodied mouth turns into a grimace and the eyes burn brighter. It hurls the marble at me.

I flinch and brace myself but the marble stops and hovers an inch from my face. The center churns with a tiny crimson fire.

The shadowy creature is nowhere to be seen but the room is in chaos as the furniture is pressed against the walls. The gales burst with hurricane force and yet I stand my ground.

Then that deep voice speaks and I feel the hate seeping from its words.

"Do you think that you could deny me your soul? I told you it's mine and you can't defy me. I'm a hunter of souls and like those I've dined on before, I will have yours. You were sold out. There is nothing you can do about it."

"I don't understand…"

"Your family has paid well for the sin of your first American born ancestor. Look deep inside the stone and you'll see him swimming in my private lake in hell, fulfilling his contract."

A twisted cackling fills the air and then its booming voice filled my head. "His name was George Monroe, my whore. I found him dying from a snake bite after he killed someone for their gold. He prayed to your God but it did no good, it never does. Then he prayed for anyone to save him."

The voice grows quieter, almost to a whisper. "I came to him just minutes from death and made him an offer. A contract that I save his life and give him 2 sacks full of gold nuggets and anything he wanted. All he had to do was let me have the souls of each first born male in his bloodline. When he saw the gold nuggets he didn't care what he signed away."

Within the marble there were several men burning in the lake. Their flesh peeled from their bodies and then healed just to burn again. This is where the howls of agony that trail this thing's laughter are coming from.

"Sin will make your soul tender and juicy. I give you the chance to enjoy what little life you have left or I could just have it now, it's all up to you."

"No. you'll never have my soul."

"No? How dare you refuse me what is already mine? I have been alive for thousands and thousands of years devouring pathetic souls just like yours, and you think that you can stop me?"

A feminine voice begins singing. "Hush little baby, don't say a word, momma's going to buy you a mocking bird…" It is hard to remember but that sounds like the voice of my mother.

The house begins to rumble. The cabinets in the kitchen open and slam shut. Silverware, cups, glasses, knives, and chairs fly around the kitchen. Everything is pulverized against the walls but nothing crosses the arch connecting the rooms.

The musical voice continues as my tears dry in the unnatural wind storm. The dark laughter returns and my bones vibrate in sync with each rumble of the horrible sound.

My mother used to sing that to me when she tucked me in every night before she died. My last memory was of her singing me to sleep with that exact song. She wrapped her arms around me as I fell asleep, singing softly into my ear. When I woke the next morning, she had left and never returned.

This is a trick. This demon tarnishes the memories of my mother. How dare it sing that song in her voice? This demon will not be dining on my soul tonight.

The anger swells inside me and I force myself to kneel. As my knee presses into the floor, I realize I am in control. Without wasting any more time thinking, I pray for protection, not just for myself but for Grandma.

Warmth spreads from my chest to my limbs as I silently pray that God forgive me for my weakness. "I am not worthy," is all that is audible.

Despite the buffeting winds, the warmth continues to move throughout my body and the miniature hurricane no longer holds me in place. I rise to my feet and raise my arms towards the ceiling and the heavens beyond.

"In the name and blood of Jesus Christ, you shall leave from here and go back to hell where you came from and never return to plague my family or any other family ever again!"

In a burst of blue flames the fiery eyes reappear but not surrounded by the shadowy darkness. The couch nearby begins to smoke as the temperature rises drastically.

The flames lower and shrink, sinking into the exposed and empty ribcage of the creature. It hunches down from its height, leaning towards me as two giant wings spread across the ceiling, glowing with fire. Everywhere they brush they leave black smears.

The misshapen head is skinless, rotten, and bleeding. The fire burns bright as the brow creases inward. The black lipless mouth peels back to reveal three narrow rows of razor edges where the teeth should have been. The cranium is topped with a pair of black horns and a trail of black spikes that run down its neck and along its spine.

The skeletal chest burns with blue flames. Thousands of fiery flies buzz in its ribs, safe from the wind. The demon shifts its huge bulky long scaled body on four thick legs each ending with a twisted foot with a various number of toes.

The warmth grows inside me and with it my strength. My fear is gone and I stand my ground with complete confidence that no evil can touch me.

Its decayed breath brushes across my nose and the demon's voice rumbles. "Do you think that I'm afraid of you or your weak little prayers? You are mine and so are the sons of your future generations."

"I'm not afraid of you or your threats because I'm armed with the Word of God and you're finished here!"

Suddenly the blue flames turn red and the wind slams into me. The furniture lifts off the floor and zooms toward the wall behind me. The windows explode as the couch crashes against them.

The demon grins at me and leans closer. "I'm glad you're not running away like a scared little dog. I want you to stay and play! I don't get to play very often."

The demon shakes while his horns gouge the low ceiling. Words fly from his mouth in a language I do not recognize. The noise sounds like my Latin professor speaking backwards.

With every syllable, the house rumbles. The walls and ceiling peel like an orange. In seconds, the entire house is ripped away leaving the floor. Where there should be fields and sky there is only the gray stone of a giant cavern. Piled and scattered against the walls are hundreds of headless skeletons. Shadowy memories fire off in my head as if I had been here before but each one I focus on just fades.

From the shadows of the cave walls, several reddish creatures emerge. With short leathery wings and burning eyes, they are miniature versions of the larger demon. The beast looms over me with a sneer on his bloody face.

"Do you recognize my lovely home?"

I have no trouble finding my voice this time. My will to resist this creature gets stronger with every breath of sulfuric air. "Don't get used to being here because I'm going to send you back to hell for all the pain and sorrow you caused my family and anyone else you destroyed!"

Turning to the smaller demons approaching me I shout. "By my Father in Heaven I command y'all into the fiery pits of hell and never return."

The cavern fills with rumbling cackles as the huge demon shakes with amusement.

"I'll find other demons and send them to hell as well!"

The demon reaches for me but he hesitates as a little demon begins to scream and clutch at its chest. Then the others soon cry out with it. They howl in agony as they engulf in flames and then explode. Little clouds of ash drift to the ground.

The huge demon steps back with his great horned head whipping around to witness the massacre. His flaming eyes are wider when he turns to me, no longer smiling.

"You… you don't have the ability to destroy me or my minions, how?"

It was my turn to smile. "With him, all things are possible if you have faith and I have faith enough to destroy you demon!"

The fear I thought I saw in him vanishes. He laughs with the screams of people burning in his tiny lake. The ground beneath me trembles and cracks.

Blood oozes from the fractures and drips down the walls from fissures spreading across the vast walls. Several holes burst open and blood pours to the floor.

The booming laughter continues as the blood edges

around the floor. It creeps towards me until it creates a circle to trap me.

Crimson liquid burns and boils around me. The demon's body quakes as the burning gaze bores into me. Does it plan to drown me with this blood or boil me? I should be afraid but I am not.

I will not let this demon get me angry. "My faith holds, demon! With the help of God, I'll destroy you once and for all. I give you one chance to go to hell on your own, or go in pieces."

Feeling a tug from inside me, I step towards the demon. The dry circle shrinks to merely inches from my bare feet. I do not hesitate and step into the blood. The burning fluid melts away from my foot before it touches the ground.

Glaring into the fiery gaze of the demon towering over me, his laughter cuts off abruptly and he roars as the blood encircles my feet without touching me.

His booming stony voice echoes throughout the cavern like a choir of angry demons. "No! No! His soul belongs to me! His ancestor made a deal with me and it's mine to collect! I have been waiting for it since he was born and he is mine and you cannot have it! You have no right to it!" The demon continues to bellow at the ceiling in that backwards Latin sounding language.

I interrupt its ranting. "Your only right is to go to hell, you foul piece of crap."

The flames burning in its ribcage turn blue. It draws a small black bladed broadsword from under its ribs. Horrible laughter fills the cavern almost as if the sound waves were trying to force me on my knees. Little fiery runes light the blade as the sword extends untill it is as long as I am. The blade bursts into flames as it expands to match the size of the demon.

I hold onto my faith with all my might as the beast shifts his bulky body and raises the sword above his head. He hesitates and stops laughing for a moment. His gaze is fixated on my eyes. "I will have your soul as you take your last breath, you pathetic worm! It is my right."

The flaming blade passes directly between my eyes and down the length of my spine before the tip embeds itself in the floor between my feet. Instead of the pain I would have expected from being cut in two, I felt a slight electric shock as the blade had passed through me.

I am whole. My clothes are not singed nor cut. I almost want to laugh at the foul demon but I hold it in.

The eyes grow larger and its pitch black mouth hangs open as it steps back from me. It releases the grip on the sword as it moves away. I step around the smoking sword jammed tightly into the floor.

"How? How did you do that?" The fear in the demon's voice is unexpected but I stay focused on what is happening and it is a lot more than I alone could do. The warmth in my chest was not coming from me, it was channeling into me. I am being used as a vessel by an outside force. All of the blood evaporates in clouds of misty red steam.

"With God on my side nothing can hurt me."

A soft warm light then surrounds me and before the demon can turn, the light seizes him like a child might grab a toy. He wails in that strange language as he struggles with the light. The flames in his chest snuff out, revealing the skeletal remnants of dozens of humans stacked inside. There are so many, it was as if there is a skeleton for every soul he has ever consumed.

The demon tries to wave off the light as it envelopes him. The fire in his eyes fades, leaving steaming sockets. His body shrivels and shrinks.

Its eyeless gaze falls upon me again and he roars as a wreath of flames appears behind the pitiful creature. It claws the ground for some kind of hold as it is sucked into the doorway. The demon and doorway vanish in a flash of light.

The demon survives. I do not understand how it is I

know for sure, but I do. He will suffer at the hands of other demons in his weakened state but he will survive. The light slowly fades. The warmth begins to cool but I feel strong.

Glaring at where the flaming wreath of a doorway was. "It will do you no good to run because I know what I have to do with my life. I will be a protector of those who need help. With God on my side I will defeat every demon just as you were defeated by us."

The sword falls to the floor as it shrinks to four feet, no longer trapped in the floor and small enough for me to hold. "Lord, if this is the path that I must take, then I accept and through my faith I will serve you!" I lift the sword to the ceiling.

As I stare at the black sword a single white feather falls from the shadows of the ceiling and floats onto the tip. The feather melts into the blade and the black metal fades to gray and then white within seconds. Lowering the weapon to get a better view, I realize the weight of it must be half of what it was when I lifted it.

A roar fills the cave. The floor shudders with footsteps approaching me from behind. I turn to the wrinkled demon. Without the flames, the massive frame still towers at more than twice my height. "I will tear your body apart and I will feed on your soul!"

"Do you not get it? Your soul eating days are done! God has a plan for me. I will save souls and keep them from demons like you."

The demon is an eyeless mask of rage. It draws near, the blue flames spark to life in the pits of its eyes but still too dim to shine beyond the sockets. It seems to grow in strength as it nears me. If the demon takes my soul, it could regain its entire strength.

The demon bellows. "I'll not be denied my supper!"

"From now on you eat in hell, for God is my salvation and through him I will defeat you!"

"I will have my revenge upon you for this humiliation

and when I am done picking your bones clean I will pay a visit to your Grandmother."

My heart leaps at those words as the smell of sulfur and rotten flesh fill my nostrils. I fight the sudden urge to vomit as the putrid smell makes my eyes water.

"No, I cast you out in the name of Jesus! To hell with you demon!"

Raising the newly reformed sword with both hands, I swing as hard as I can towards his head. The demon halts his advance and his eye sockets expand. His jaw hangs awkwardly to the side as charcoal dust pours down his neck. His expression is frozen when his head falls from the neck. The massive horns clatter on the floor as the misshapen orb bounces past me. The body hardens and cracks. It crumbles until there is nothing but a pile of dust that shrinks until nothing is left but an ashy stain on the cave floor.

I kneel to pray. "Lord, thank you for bestowing this honor upon me so that I can do your work and spread your 'Word' of faith."

Opening my eyes, I have to remind myself to breathe. Everything is where it is supposed to be. The couch is against the wall, the windows were intact and closed. Not a single dust bunny was disturbed.

Was it all a dream? My gaze drifts to the weight in my right hand and I realize that it was not. The white shiny sword is in my grip. I blink at the weapon as it looks smaller than a moment ago. No, I am not imagining things; it is shrinking until it is the size of a pendant. The words 'Hope' and 'Faith' are inscribed on each side of the tiny blade.

I carefully slip the sharp little blade into my pocket without jabbing myself. Plopping on the couch, I catch my breath. A sigh escapes my lips as I hear rolling under the couch.

Leaning forward to get a look, my heart stutters as a little red marble rolls from under the couch between my feet. It steadily moves halfway across the floor before it pops into a cloud of smoke.

Sorting my thoughts as I lean my head back has never been so difficult. What is real? Was I dreaming or did I fight a real demon? A sharp prickly sensation on my chest reminds me of the pendant. I was not dreaming then. Or I am trapped in the dream. I can smell the sulfurous smoke released from the marble.

COCK-A-DOODLE-DOO!

My ears are instantly ringing from the sound of Jack Sparks announcing the morning before the sun had risen. Turning my head in the direction of his alarm, I come nose to beak with him.

"Did you really have to do that right now?"

Then I notice the sun light pouring in and warming me. Making eye contact with Jack, his response is a light cackle sound as if he thought the whole routine was funny somehow. That is enough proof for me that chickens have a sense of humor.

From the kitchen, a warm familiar voice calls to me. "Are you going to sleep all morning or are you going to get up and come eat breakfast?"

Without taking my attention from Jack, I reply. "I think we should have fried chicken for dinner tonight." I smile at Jack Sparks but somehow he understands because he jumps from the couch and flaps out the open window. Then he flies off the porch and runs across the yard to the coops.

It feels good to laugh this morning but my stomach is refusing to go along until it is filled with the delicious breakfast that I smell. I rush into the kitchen and sit as Grandma places my plate in front of me, stacked with buttered pancakes, flanked by scrambled eggs and a pile of bacon.

"Now you eat and I will be right back. I'll have something for you when I get back."

"Ok, Grandma."

I was swallowing my third bite as Grandma returns with that journal from the box. She waves it at me to take it.

"This is for you. It may have some answers for you. I really don't know because I've never opened it." She says as I accept it from her.

"What do you mean, answers?"

"The dark figure you dreamed about, well it wasn't really a dream. It was as real as can be. It was a demon that's been killing the men of this family. Sometimes it took them when they were young, other times it took them when they were older but it always took them in their sleep."

The pancake catches in my throat and I have to swallow another bite to shove it down before asking. "How did you know?"

"My grandfather told me what he was going through and what to do with the box. That night he died in his sleep and then he was cremated that day and nobody got to view his body except for Mom. All these years I have been terrified that you would be taken from me before you had the strength to beat the demon. The moment you told me that you wanted to be a priest I knew that you could do it. I hope you'll be ready when he comes for you."

"Grandma, I love you."

It does not matter to me that God has chosen a more difficult path for me than joining the priesthood. I am not going to tell her that either so long as she knows that I serve him.

I scoot the plate of half eaten food to the side and lay the journal in front of me. My stomach protests but I must read this.

The inside cover has scribbles with barely legible handwriting.

'To my kinfolk,

Read this and please be aware that once you open the door, you can never close it.'

"Yes you can, all you need is faith." I say to the book with a shake of my head.

Flipping through the journal, I read about my Great-Great Grandfather and his dreams and dealings with the demon. How he discovered the truth behind the deaths of the men in the family. After I finish reading, I flip to the last page and finish the story.

'I, Adam Monroe, am the last to write in this journal. The family curse has ended and I will start a new journal as a defender against demons and their minions. Against the tides of evil that smother this world, I will stand as a beacon in the name of the Lord. I will burn the darkness as a wildfire of light.'
The End. Or is it?

I Never Was And Always Will Be

I never was anything to anyone and I never will be any more than that. I tried to be more than you thought. I could be more but you told me I was nothing and then you laughed. I can never be more than I am and I am tired of trying. I am just tired of waiting for the moon to rise. The dreams that I dream at midnight are the dreams that I should have dreamt before I went to sleep, but now is the time for clouds to cover the stars as my mind whispers in my ears. My voice drowns with thoughts as the rain falls up into the clouds of my mind. It reminds me that I never was or ever will be any more than I am. Never look back at me because I am there no longer but I will always be here in the past where you have put me. Now you can walk to where I have never been. If you want to see me just close your eyes and remember where was and I will always be here waiting where you left me and where my dreams are buried.

AUTHOR'S NOTE

My name is John Alba but my friends call me JP. I grew up in what was once a very small town but now it is a very big town called Round Rock, Texas. The town is really named after a round rock. I was raised by great parents and I am the oldest of three brothers and no sisters but lots of family. I am married with three kids. I like to collect anything toy related, antiques, or anything collectible. I love ghost stories, horror movies, westerns, comedies, and all kinds of movies. I have had all kinds of jobs like a janitor, fast food, postal, government, and state employment and many more.

I am "A jack of all trades and master of none." Most of my life's woes I have forgotten but the ones I do remember made me who I am today. From an early age I can remember thinking of what would happen if I did this or if I did that. I was a worry wart. Always thinking about what would go wrong if I threw a rock high in the air or if I would ride my bicycle over a ramp or is there such a thing as a balding porcupine? Stuff like that.

When I turned eight or nine my mind would not shut up when I tried to go to sleep. It would ramble about what I did or didn't do that day or what I said or didn't say. Then once I finished with doing all that my mind would start on the next day with "what if this happened or if that happened" and so on and so on.

It wasn't until I was fourteen years old when I learned to focus on stuff I wanted to think about. Although my mind still didn't shut up. That is when I started to create stories so that my head would not be so chaotic. My imagination created stories so well that it was like watching a movie and I was the director.

My mind was not always so willing to give up its power and that is why I write stories on paper. I would see a story in my head and write it as fast as possible. I do not sit and think about what I should write (although sometimes I get to pick the premise of the story.) My mind shows me what to write and I try to keep up. Sometimes there is too much stuff. In the last twenty five years my mind has been showing me things while I least expect it, even when I am fully awake. I can't stop it; I can only hold it off until I am ready to write it down. Either way, here I am telling you my thoughts and here you are reading my mind.

Welcome to my imagination...

To all the ones that opened their mind to me, thank you for letting me play in your head, scare you later.